♥ Heart on Fire ♥

A Romance

by

WILLIAM MALTESE

WRITING AS "WILLA LAMBERT"

The Borgo Press
An Imprint of Wildside Press

MMVII

♥ _Contents_ ♥

Chapter One..7
Chapter Two 17
Chapter Three 25
Chapter Four...37
Chapter Five 51
Chapter Six...61
Chapter Seven 71
Chapter Eight..81
Chapter Nine...91
Chapter Ten 105
Chapter Eleven 113
Chapter Twelve 115
Chapter Thirteen..117
Chapter Fourteen 127
Chapter Fifteen 131
Chapter Sixteen 133
Chapter Seventeen..135
Chapter Eighteen 137
Chapter Nineteen..139
Chapter Twenty 141

♥ *<u>Heart on Fire</u>* ♥

♥ *Chapter One* ♥

"I DO WISH YOU'D RECONSIDER this Mt. St. Helens business," Grace Woof said to her daughter. "Who knows when it'll explode again? You? The scientists who didn't have a clue the first time?"

"They're monitoring the mountain more closely, these days," Janine argued, for not the first time. "I'll be fine. Besides, I need something to keep me occupied until Marine World gets refurbished after the fire. You want me hanging around here, all of the time, and making a nuisance of myself?"

Grace shook her head at the ridiculous suggestion that her daughter would ever be a nuisance. "You know we'd love to see more of you."

"Look how this allows me to take advantage of your having insisted I minor in Home Economics." Janine knew her mother's purpose in *that* had really been for her daughter to prepare for married life, not so that Janine could go off and cook for some scientific team ensconced on a mountain that had already blown once and could very well blow again.

"Janine will be fine," her father told his wife and put his daughter's suitcase directly to the side of the front door.

Mack Woof was a large, well-built man who laughed easily. He'd gone to WSU on a football scholarship, and he'd led his first-string team to a number of astounding victories. He could have turned pro—had even gotten several fat-cat offers—but Grace hadn't seen having a professional football player for a husband as any way *she* wanted to live. Professional football locker rooms were afloat with cocaine and steroids and other illegal drugs, and that wasn't the ideal atmosphere for any husband of hers. In the end, Mack had agreed. Besides, he'd always loved Grace more than he'd loved knocking around other guys on the football field. He now made a good living as head of the three grocery stores Grace had inherited from her father, and he was quick to remind that had he stuck to the sport he'd probably, by now, be laid up with a bum knee, with nothing whatsoever else to show for it.

"What if you should need a doctor for some reason?" Grace wanted Janine to answer *that* all-important question for her.

"There's a medical doctor on site, and a good one, too. Hank Heidelburg was on-call when I worked at the Department of Fisheries that one summer. There's, also, a helicopter for emergency medical evac."

"A lot of people are surprised to hear you're leaving so soon." Grace was as prepared to wrestle with the subject as the family dog liked to wrestle a bone. "I spent weeks bragging up the fact that my youngest daughter was going to be home for the summer, and here she is, up and leaving before she's even settled in."

Janine shifted her position to see a portion of the backyard through the open verandah doors.

She spotted Dr. *("Please, call me Chad!")* Samuels. He had this positively marvelous mane of lion's-gold hair that made him hard to miss in the sea of predominantly Italian family-Woof. There was something aesthetically pleasing about any blond, male or female, who tanned well, probably because light-haired people were so much more likely to turn lobster red and peel.

Janine wondered where "Lou" had gotten off to. Luella (Lou) Gessler, an old friend and college roommate, was the one who'd recommended Janine for kitchen supervisor when the job had unexpectedly become available on the mountain.

Janine hadn't expected Lou to have Dr. Samuels… Chad…in tow when Lou had turned up with him that afternoon on the Woof doorstep. According to Lou, Chad had been in Spokane on personal business and had needed a ride back to the mountain.

"Be sure to say good-bye to your Great-Grandma Woof," Grace reminded Janine and interrupted her daughter's train of thought. "She's ninety-one, after all, and none of us know just long she's going to be with us."

The insinuation was that Great-Grandma Woof was most likely going to drop dead while Janine was off on the mountain.

"Of course, I will." Janine had hoped to just fade away and not undergo the last-minute scrutiny Great-Grandma Woof would provide as regarded the man suddenly joining Janine and Lou in their ride up the assumedly dreaded Washington-state volcano.

She headed in Chad's direction and was intercepted by Uncle Joseph who wanted her to have a hamburger. She didn't want one, thank you.

"Here, try my new recipe for bread-and-butter pickles!" insisted Aunt Betty who'd apparently brought some of her own food to supplement the overflowing supply Grace had balanced precariously on every conceivable flat surface.

"Delicious," Janine complimented, escaping with her mouthful.

At this rate, neither she, nor Lou, nor poor Dr. (Chad) Samuels would make it out the door before the next morning.

"Off to Mt. St. Helens, I hear," said brother-in-law Gerald. He'd been a line-backer at Idaho State, and there was no way Janine was going to get by him without a good deal of clever faking and footwork. Luckily, little Trent-Talbot chose that particular moment to spill 7-Up on Aunt Gloria, and daddy Gerald had to go play referee.

"Sorry about all of this," Janine managed, rather breathlessly, when she miraculously, *finally*, arrived at her intended destination.

Dr. Chad Samuels's eyes, whose glance meet hers, were the color of rich amber that had petrified from prehistoric pitch, and there were sunbursts of jet exploding outward from the shade-dilated pupil of each one.

His hair, and tan, dimples, eyes, nose, and full mouth with its faint crinkles at its corners, all just went perfectly together.

Lou was dark-complexioned and less noticeable in her chair directly next to her fellow scientist.

"We can leave any time, you guys," Janine said, then added upon noticing that her mother was noticing, "just as soon as I say my official good-bye to the family matriarch."

"She's holding court in the pavilion," Lou said. Having roomed with Janine in school, she'd been subjected to several of these large family gatherings and was less at sea in this one than Chad so obviously was.

Chad took another bite of the heaping pile of potato salad earlier forced upon him by one Janine's aunts, or cousins; he couldn't remember who, except that the woman had an exceptional head of ebony-black hair.

"This should only take a minute," Janine blatantly lied and headed off toward Great-Grandma Woof.

"Scientists make a good deal of money, do they?" Great-Grandma Woof greeted Janine from her rocking chair, first unceremoniously shooing off an assortment of grandchildren, great-grandchildren, and the like. "I only ask, because I don't see scientist *you* living in any mansion at the moment and riding around in a Mercedes-Benz."

Janine knew Great-Grandma Woof's comment had little to do with Janine, a lot to do with Dr. Chad Samuels.

"Lou says he has a very large trust fund." Janine wondered if that would meet with the old lady's approval, or....

"He's suspiciously too handsome to be a scientist," observed Great-Grandma Woof. "He's suspiciously too handsome to be a man. Do you think he's gay?"

"I haven't a clue." Janine could only hope Chad Samuels *wasn't* gay. Leave it to Great-Grandma Woof

11

to taint Janine's delight in having, for the first time, in a very long time, finally found a truly good-looking male of the species.

"Handsome men can be truly charming, but ugly men make the best husbands," Great-Grandma Woof observed. "Keep that in mind while you're off impressing *him* with your cooking."

Speaking of impressive, Great-Grandma Woof was certainly that. She sat ramrod straight, bedecked in a conservatively cut dress of blue-black cotton and lace that looked nonetheless in fashion for having been homespun and home-sewn over half a century before. Her once-black hair, long gone pure white, was dyed black, but there was still a lot of it, all tucked precisely into a large bun atop her head and held there by massive hair pins.

She didn't look nearly as old as she was, although her porcelain skin was finally beginning to show wrinkles that resembled the crackling on fine China.

"Did he say his family was from Sweden, or Norway?"

Janine didn't have a clue.

Great-Grandma Woof's eyes were the same bright blue as they'd been when she'd first spotted Brigham Woof across the lawn of another party so many years before.

"It might be every interesting to see what kind of children would result from his blond good looks and your dark complexion."

"Dr. Samuels is *an associate*, Great-Grandma," Janine chided. "Not even that, really. This project will see me stuck in the kitchen and likely not even seeing him except at meals."

"You do know that this mountain of yours could catastrophically burn down the rest of itself just as easily as that other place you worked?"

Janine could still shudder at what had happened at Marine World. Namu-Six, their popular killer whale, had been caught in a small holding tank when the fire broke out. Staff and fire fighters had tried to open the gate to the sea, but the winch had malfunctioned. After which, Namu-Six had come to the surface once too often into blast-furnace conditions. Environmentalists were still up in arms.

"You expecting to find a replacement orca for Namu-Six up on that mountain?" Great-Grandma Woof asked, the twinkle increasing in her blue eyes. "You *are* a fish biologist, isn't that what your mother told me? If Namu-Six got fried in a little fire, what do you think happened to all of those poor little fishes in all of those mountain streams and lakes when St. Helens blew its whole top?"

"Whatever, it'll be the concern of Lou and Dr. Samuels and the other scientists, while I peel their potatoes and boil their water."

"You're a good cook, are you? Men do like women who can cook." Great-Grandma settled back in her chair and pulled her shawl closer around her in spite of the warmth of the afternoon. "Men like women who are attractive. You're certainly that."

Janine had a thick mane of Woof black hair (there wasn't mention of a bald Woof in the annals of Woof genealogy—which was traced back to Charlemagne on her father's side and to Cimabue on her mother's side). She had nicely shaped eyebrows over a pair of striking, wide-set blue eyes. In fact, her eyes were probably her best feature, although more than one boyfriend had commented on her "cute" nose.

Her lips and body were full and, to Great-Grandma's notion, a mite *too* sensuous, in that they reminded the matriarch of Lady Abitha de Woof whose only surviving image was a miniature painted on a now-antique ivory broach kept secured with several other family heirlooms in a safety deposit box at the Dishman branch of the Washington Trust Bank. Lady Abitha's affairs, political and otherwise, in the court of England's King Henry VIII, were some of several skeletons found rattling in the Woof closet. By Janine's age, Lady Abitha had gone through four husbands, three dead by mysterious circumstances, and had given birth to three bastards. By contrast, Janine seemed destined to reach old age without giving marriage or childbirth even one go-round.

"So, just why *aren't* you married?" asked Great-Grandma for not the first time. "I forget."

Janine shrugged. It was the easiest line of self-defense. She didn't *know* why, except that there just hadn't been anyone for her like there had been for just about everyone else in the family.

"You know where Troutdale is up on that mountain of yours?" Great-Grandma asked. "Really close to this camp of yours, as I understand it."

"Really close as the crow flies," Janine reminded. Distances in wilderness areas were deceptive.

"Close enough for you to visit, I would think, yes? In that, I've this old friend of mine presently living there, Sarah Zent, and I'd like you to stop by and say hello as soon as you can squeeze in a minute or two of your time, between peeling all of those potatoes and boiling all of that water."

"Sure, I can do that," Janine assured. In reality, what with three meals to be served, each and every day, she didn't think she'd have many spare moments, but she wasn't about to tell Great-Grandma Woof that.

Heart on Fire, by William Maltese

♥ *Chapter Two* ♥

"**SO, ALL OF THOSE REALLY *WERE***
Woofs?" Chad asked; Lou steered the car left on Sprague Avenue and headed them for the ramp accessing the freeway.

"Or *married to* Woofs, or *descended from* Woofs, or *related to* Woofs," Janine elucidated. "There was more than a fair representation of mom's side of the family, too."

"That would be the Farnwells," Lou said and eyed Chad in the rearview mirror; he'd taken advantage of the extra leg room in the back seat, both women in front.

They drove in silence for a couple of minutes, Lou changing to an outside lane to pass an Idaho-licensed camper before announcing, "You do know, Chad, that all of those Woofs and Farnwells are hot to find out why this particular Miss Woof, riding with us here, is so long in linking up with some Mr. Right."

Janine's blush made her cheeks go pink. "I really doubt Chad is interested in any of that."

"Why wouldn't he be interested?" Lou provided a wide smile. If she caught the daggers Janine's eyes were throwing, she chose to ignore them.

"*You* just pay more attention to the road, please," Janine insisted.

"Lou," injected Chad, "is just so happy about Jack and her relationship, these days, that she seems intent upon pairing up just about everybody else." He tried to shift to a more comfortable position.

"Jack?" Janine didn't miss her cue.

"Jack Ledben," Chad obliged. "Don't tell me Lou hasn't mentioned him to you. He's our team geochemist to whom, we all suspect, Lou has been giving a crash course in advanced biology."

"Tacky!" Lou accused.

"And why is this the first time I've heard anything about this Jack?" Janine wanted to know.

"Probably because telling you would have made what I have going with him seem way too serious," Lou confessed. "Besides, I was *going* to tell you— *after* you got settled in on the mountain."

"Then, it's not serious between you and him, huh?" Chad carried on. "You could have fooled me and everyone else."

"Jack and I have agreed to keep our relationship *light,*" Lou explained.

"As opposed to what?" Chad wanted to know. *"Heavy?"*

Janine was glad he was keeping the conversation moving so she didn't have to.

"Jack and I are going to play it by ear," Lou added.

"Hmmmmmm." Chad sounded dubious.

"Enough!" Lou insisted. "I don't want you to give Janine the wrong impression."

"Or the *right* impression," Chad mused under his breath.

"I'll fill you in on Jack later, Janine, promise." Lou smiled. "You'll like him."

If Lou had finally found someone, Janine was happy for her. Lou had been looking as long as Janine, except for Lou's unfortunate four-month relationship with Jeff Potter when they were all in their junior year at WSU. Janine hadn't liked Jeff. Before that mess was over, Lou had found him out, too, and didn't like him any more than Janine did. There had been some pretty scary tightrope walking there for awhile. Janine had wondered, more than once, at the time, if her and her roommate's friendship was going to survive it. Luckily, it had only grown stronger.

On the other hand, if Lou had found someone, Janine couldn't help being a little jealous. Certainly, there remained no one special on Janine's immediate horizon. Maybe she was destined to be an old maid after all.

"You know?" Chad said a few minutes later, leaning his forearms up on the front seat between Lou and Janine. His face was so close to Janine, she could smell the tartness of his lime-based cologne. "I'm a little envious of Janine and all her aunts, uncles, cousins, nieces, nephews, brothers, and sisters. I used to fantasize being part of a big family."

"I always knew you *had* to be an only child." Lou welcomed the shift in conversation. "You have that air of one-and-only about you."

"Have you been in Spokane, then, visiting your parents, Chad?" Janine asked, interested in what had brought him down from the mountain.

"I had to clear up some family legal business. Since Lou was scheduled to pick you up and drive the both of you back to St. Helens, she's letting me—thank-you very much!—tag along for the ride."

"And we're happy to have him along, aren't we, Janine?" Lou chimed in, increasing pressure on the gas to pass a semi in the right-hand lane.

Who wouldn't be happy to have Chad along? He was pleasant, charming—and handsome. He was a colleague, and he would be working in the same scientific camp as Janine—if in an admittedly different capacity than her dealings in the kitchen. It was nice to get to meet another member of the team, besides Lou and Dr. Hank Heidelburg. Still, there was something about Chad that made her uneasy, if not in an unpleasant kind of way. She couldn't remember getting quite the same feeling from meeting anyone else, and she was at a loss to explain it away.

Janine only wished she knew Dr. Roger Lewis who had been appointed by the U.S. Geological Society to head the work team of scientists now on the mountain. Lou had talked Dr. Lewis into taking on Janine, sight unseen, when Barry Wilcox almost lost his arm as a result of a well-aimed swat from a massive bear. Lou had argued that it couldn't hurt to have another biologist in reserve, albeit in the kitchen, just in case things started happening. Still unpredictable, Mt. St. Helens could start up again, at any time, and cause a lot of excitement, although it was doubtful it could match its display of May 1980 when it blew off

1,300 feet of its crest and devastated 200 square miles of Washington State.

Lou steered the car into the first off-ramp that accessed a rest area.

"I thought this was going to be a drive straight through," Chad joked. Actually, he had to go to the toilet, too, all of the bathrooms at Janine's having been filled non-stop with a steady line of Woofs and Farnwells.

Lou took the next curve at a speed that shifted Janine toward the door.

"You must *really* have to go," Chad shouted after Lou who was quickly out the door and running as soon as the car pulled to an abrupt stop

Janine laughed, unfastened her seat belt and got out. Momentarily, she contemplated joining Lou in the restroom, but didn't. She'd been luckier in getting to a toilet at her parents' house; part of a big family, she'd grown used to diplomatically maneuvering to the front of any line.

Chad did follow Lou, at least until he detoured to the men's room. He was back before Lou reappeared.

"Lou says you're a biologist, as well as a cook," he said upon joining Janine. "Interesting career combination—biology and cooking."

"My mother insisted I at least minor in Home Economics. She's convinced the scientific world is only filled with old men more interested in test tubes than in women."

Chad laughed; Janine wondered if he knew she'd been about to comment upon how he'd proved her mother's theory completely wrong.

"You were at Marine World until the fire?" He sounded unsure.

"Right," she admitted.

"I know Curt Simms. Worked with him a short while on stream-fed hot pools down around Lassen."

"Curt is a nice guy." Janine would never forget how touched she'd been when he'd broken down and cried when the winch malfunctioned, and they'd all known for sure Namu-Six didn't have a chance of surviving the holocaust.

"Nasty fire you people had there. Still on schedule for reopening this fall?"

"Last I heard. Repairs seem to be coming along as projected, but the environmentalists are putting up a fuss about letting us bring in another killer whale. 'Couldn't even keep safe the one they had!' they're screaming." She shook her head. She was as much for preserving the ecology as the next person, probably more so, but she couldn't fathom the reasoning of some very well-meaning people. How many men, women, and children would never know the wonder of seeing an orca up close and personal if all the whales were left swimming far out at sea? There had to be compromises made somewhere along the line.

"Okay, people, pit-stop over," Lou said, looking far more at ease than when she'd hurriedly left them.

"You want me to drive for awhile?" Janine volunteered.

"Sure," Lou conceded. Once in the car, she gave every indication that she planned to take every advantage to catch some shut-eye.

"When you get tired, let me know," Chad said and smiled at Janine via his reflection available upfront in the rearview mirror.

He was particularly handsome when he smiled.

HEART ON FIRE, BY WILLIAM MALTESE

♥ *Chapter Three* ♥

"I THINK HE MIGHT NEED some help," Janine said. "What do you think?"

They had been stopped by rocks on the night-black dirt logging road that led to the camp higher up the slope of Mt. St. Helens. Most of the stones had already been dispensed with by Chad, but the last one looked as if it would take even more strength than even his impressive physique could muster. Unfortunately, the boulder in question sat dead-center the road, leaving the car insufficient room to squeeze by on either side.

"Think we should give Hercules a hand, do you?" Lou asked. She and Janine already had their car doors open and were stepping out.

The women added their shoulders to Chad's at the massive obstacle. It showed no response whatsoever to their combined efforts.

"I think we have a bit more, here, than we can chew," Lou ventured. "This might call for the bull-dozer from camp, rather than we three mortals."

"Easier said than done," Chad reminded. "Cell phone reception is nonexistent up here, or have you forgotten?"

"How far is it, walking?" Janine asked and looked up as more gravel dislodged somewhere above them and began a disconcerting slide that stopped somewhere with in the concealing underbrush.

"It might be easier to drive back to Cougar and spend the night there," Lou said. "We can radio from there and have one of the guys come down with the bulldozer to let us on through."

"You're telling me the three of us can't handle this problem without a bulldozer?" Chad asked.

"Yes, that *is* what I'm suggesting," Lou admitted.

"Possibly, you're right," Chad surprised.

"So, it's back to Cougar, then, is it?" Janine asked.

There was a sudden sound of something very large, and very fast-moving, coming at them through the nearby trees and shrubbery. The sound faded as quickly as it had begun.

"If that's the bear that put the previous cook in the hospital, I'd feel safer inside the car," Janine admitted.

Several birds squawked and fluttered to flight before quickly returning to their roosts.

"I say we head back to Cougar and repeat this leg of the trip after someone makes it a little easier for us," Lou voted again.

"Obviously, you never learned much about fulcrums and levers in physics," Chad said with a new note of confidence. He pointed to a rectangular block of rock not far off the roadway. "Fulcrum," he said. He pointed toward a fence-post sized tree trunk that had been sawed off and left nearby, either during the logging road's original construction or, later, when the scientific team moved through. "Lever," he said, as if explaining basic physics to two high-school freshmen.

"With that rock, that piece of timber, and you two ladies in support of my efforts, the rest of this road will
be cleared in no time."

Any immediate comment by either woman was interrupted by more sounds from the underbrush. This
time it wasn't nearly as loud as before.

"Sounds as if the animals are restless tonight,"
Janine said with a nervous laugh. The moonlight,
which had originally seemed so romantic, had suddenly taken on an icy, brittle quality.

"You don't suppose they know something we
don't?" Lou asked.

"You mean, like maybe these rocks didn't just
happen to come tumbling down because of simple erosion?" Chad suggested.

Janine eyed first Lou and then Chad. Surely, neither was suggesting someone had purposely ava-
lanched the rock into the roadway.

"We haven't had the radio on, because of poor reception," Lou reminded.

"We wouldn't have needed the radio," Chad said.
"We would have felt it, don't you suppose?"

"Felt what?" Janine asked.

"The mountain still shakes a bit on occasion,"
Chad said.

Lou and he had been referring to *something* not to
someone.

Janine now knew exactly what they meant. The
idea of an earthquake shouldn't have come as any big
surprise. The area had been constantly jolted by them
prior to the May 1980 eruption, and more earthquakes
had accompanied all previous flare-ups. Earth tremors
went hand in hand with volcanic activity. However,

there was a major difference between reading about earthquakes and realizing one might strike at any moment. Janine had never been in one up to this point in her life and, although the odds were pretty good she'd be in one or more before she left this assignment on the mountain, she wasn't looking forward to it happening.

"It's probably just erosion," Chad consoled. "As for the animals, we probably disturbed them just by being here."

"Right!" Lou assured. "Now, about this boulder?"

Lou and Janine watched while Chad hauled over the rectangular-shaped stone and positioned it so it would act as the fulcrum to the pole he retrieved next. He wedged the leading end of the pole underneath the large boulder, resting a higher point on the pole against the smaller block-like stone. Lou, Janine, and Chad, pulled down on the uplifted far end of the lever, exerting the effort that would hopefully flip the boulder into a roll. Chad had calculated to take advantage of a small depression in the ground to one side of the rock, a rut made at one time by a constant flush of water over the roadway to waterfall over the steep drop-off beyond.

"You think maybe it's going to be Cougar, after all?" Lou pondered aloud when their first efforts did very little except rock the boulder.

Chad repositioned the leading end of the pole for a better "bite."

"You both have to show me more of that heave-ho women's-lib muscle of yours," Chad encouraged and spit in the palms of his hands for a better grip on the rough-barked pole.

"Whoever said I was a woman's-libber?" Lou asked and balanced herself for better leverage. "All I ever wanted was a husband and a family. This job is something to hold me over in the interim."

"I wouldn't let Roger hear you say that if I were you," Chad said with a good-natured cluck of his tongue. "Our Dr. Lewis likes to think his team is all career-oriented professionals who eat, drink, sleep, and live scientific research, private-life be damned!"

"I wouldn't let Jack Ledben hear it, either," Janine said, welcoming the opportunity to insert a dig of her own. She shouldn't have had to hear about Lou and Jack's relationship from Chad. "He might think you were contemplating him as serious husband material."

"Are you two purposely ganging up on me?" Lou asked with a chagrin more faked than real. "If you are, please stop and concentrate on getting this rock out of the roadway so I can get to bed."

"Mention Jack, and note, please, the direction—bed—in which her mind immediately heads," Chad joked.

"Kindly remember that you're in the presence of a young lady whose proper upbringing doesn't make her appreciative of your particular brand of off-color humor," Lou reminded.

"Sorry, Janine," Chad apologized good-naturedly. "It has to be you about whom she speaks. Can't be her."

"Remind me not to have you build any pyramids that I may have scheduled for construction at any time up the line," Lou said, going through the motions of pretending to operate the lever herself. The pole moved a bit, but the boulder didn't shift even a fraction of an inch. "With you on the work team, the poor cornerstone would take years and years to get laid."

"*Get laid,* did you say?" Chad asked, taking full advantage of *that* double entendre. "Thinking of Jack, again, are you?"

Lou and Janine groaned in unison.

"One…two…three! Once again, please, ladies! One…two…."

"Cougar is beginning to look more and more inviting as an alternative to slave labor," Lou said.

On their next try, though, the boulder actually moved. At first, it didn't seem likely that it was going to move any too far, but a scrunching of the ground beneath it sent the over-size rock on a half-roll half-slide that dropped it, finally, off and over the edge.

"Success!" Chad shouted congratulations to the three of them.

The boulder picked up speed on its descent and entered trees at the bottom of the grade. There was a squawk of birds, and the previously seen flock again took flight, this time as an undulating curtain that momentarily blocked the moon as fully as any complete eclipse.

Rather than circle a few times and return to their roost, this time, they circled once and veered, as one, toward the horizon.

Janine felt herself suddenly in a strange stillness broken only by the sudden slide of additional gravel from the embankment behind her. She caught the nervous looks exchanged between Lou and Chad.

"I really think we should get back in the car and drive on, now," Chad suggested.

"Just how stable is that slope, do you suppose?" Lou asked nervously, nodding toward the incline from which the boulder had obviously tumbled before they'd sent it on its merry way farther downhill.

"I'd just as soon not stick around to find out, would you?" Chad took Janine's arm and headed her toward the car.

It seemed to happen in the time it took for just one footstep. The ground heaved up, bringing both of Janine's knees to her chin. A second later, the same ground dropped away, leaving Janine seemingly suspended in midair. She'd begun the seemingly long fall, when the ground came back to her with a vengeance that knocked the breath out of her.

Her instinct for survival told her she would be better off in the car. The trouble was that she couldn't seem to find the car. When she did spot it, it was tilted precariously sideways, and there were brown ocean-like waves of land between her and it. Even Lou, whom Janine spotted, now and again, seemed to be playing hide and seek behind earth movement, rising and falling, between them.

Moving wasn't as difficult as controlling her movements when she moved. Janine might have wanted to go in one direction, but she ended up going in quite another. It was as if she were on the receiving end of a fraternity blanket-toss, except, each time she came down, there was nothing soft to catch her.

"Ouch!" Something hit her hard on the back of her head. She tried to explore the damage done, but her arms kept waving this way and that, as if she were fighting off a swarm of bees.

She…had…*no*…control!

When she realized Chad was the sudden weight on top of her, she thought the heaving earth had dumped him there. Despite his smothering bulk, she welcomed the physical contact. He was another human being sharing this trial with her, and she could derive strength and hope from his closeness. She would later remember feeling vaguely embarrassed as to just how much pleasure she took from his hard body. However, there on that road, she was too concerned with survival to pay much mind to emotions that had little to do with her possibly life-and-death situation.

"Protect your head!" she heard him order. Anyway, she thought it was his voice, seemingly confirmed by how his large hand suddenly cupped the back of her head to tuck her face securely against his chest and shoulder. She immediately smelled a heady fragrance of disturbed earth, virile man, and lime-scented cologne.

Although the ground seemed to buck less and less, Janine heard a sound reminiscent of the fist-sized hail once dropped from the sky onto her parents' home in Spokane.

Someone—she?—squealed when hit by several of whatever it was suddenly dropped, en masse, from the sky upon them.

Where *was* Lou?

Chad grunted as he, too, was hit. Janine remained unsure just what assaulted them, because Chad kept her pressed so securely against him. His every resulting moan vibrated through her as if she were a tuning fork.

There was a very loud thud close to her right ear. She tried to turn towards it, but Chad's hand kept her face wedged tightly against him. All she saw was darkness.

How long was she crushed beneath him before she realized the only sounds remaining were her and his heavy breathing? She'd later have access to the graphs and readouts from the scientific team's monitoring equipment, and those would record a 6.4 earthquake for a duration of thirty seconds. She'd go to her grave thinking it was far bigger and that it had lasted far longer.

Chad pulled himself off her. She missed the feel of him. He'd been her protective blanket against the fury of the worst. He was sprinkled with a heavy coat of dust and looked like one of those people who supposedly had their hair turn ash-grey after a major scare.

"Are you all right?" he asked her. He looked genuinely dazed and rubbed his right shoulder; his grimace told Janine something had hit him hard.

"I think so." She moved, testing the parts of her body one at a time, and judging just how well each had survived her ordeal.

"There'll be aftershocks," he warned. "We'll be safer in the car."

Janine stood up in a landscape vastly changed. A fissure had opened behind the car and now divided the roadway into two separate pieces, one on each side of a six-foot chasm. A landslide of dirt had cascaded the mountain and was tented window-height against the left side of their now-tipped car. The ground all around was pockmarked with craters where rocks, now everywhere, had barreled and bounced down the mountain. How many of those would have struck Janine if Chad hadn't been there to shield her from them?

"You're hurt!" she said; he still rubbed his shoulder and now walked with an obvious limp.

"I doubt it's serious." He was optimistic.

She finally remembered Lou and shouted her name. She looked where she'd last seen her friend, but there was nothing there but several hand-sized stones.

She looked anxiously toward the car and hoped Lou had somehow made it there, but the car was empty.

"If you two wanted a little privacy, you could have just asked me nicely to get lost." Lou wearily lifted her head above a pile of freshly deposited dirt at least six yards from where she'd begun her ride on the shifting earth. "I really think that might have been easier and a damned sight more hospitable."

"Yeah, right!" Chad helped her to her feet; she was dusted with the same fine gray powder that had sprinkled Chad and Janine and made the moon a filmy cataract eye above them.

"To the car, I think, yes?" Lou suggested. Even as she did, the ground moved again.

Janine had taken Beginning Gymnastics in college, and she knew just how walking on a trampoline felt. Except, while she could judge the give and take of stretched canvas, these troughs and peaks were too low and too high to gauge successfully.

They didn't make it to the safety of the car, but they were able to scramble against the auto and use it as a brace as well as a shield between them and the latest waterfalls of stone that tumbled the mountain.

Suffering vertigo and nausea from her inner balance system thrown temporarily for a loop, Janine again surrendered to the comfort of Chad's offered

34

arm, snuggling closer and closer to him even when all the forces of nature seemed determined to shake them apart.

Below the road, several trees that had survived the major jolt, but whose hold on earth had become tenuous, crashed to their deaths, knocking down other trees in the process.

"How many more aftershocks as powerful as that one, do you think?" Lou asked when the pause finally came.

"You tell me," Chad said; his guess as good as hers. "However many, I think we'd better move from here while the moving is still good."

The chasm had widened behind the car, actually threatening to swallow the vehicle like those much-publicized sinkholes were always gobbling up houses, along the Gulf Coast, on the prime-time news.

"Drive out?" Lou dubiously eyed the latest obstacles nature had strewn across their pathway. There was no way they could risk taking the time to clear away stones, which meant waving good-bye to her Ford's already suspect never-the-best suspension system.

"I think the more we can get over our heads, besides the black night sky and the mountain, the better off we're going to be." Chad gave a jerk on the car door. Despite its evident protests, the result of new massive denting and damage, the dirt-coated metal finally came open.

Janine had visions of the car not starting. Wasn't that the way it always happened in the movies? But the motor turned first time. Lou, who had obviously had similar fears, gave a quick prayer of thanks under her breath. Chad looked as if he were the cat who'd swallowed the canary.

"Fasten your set belts; this is going to be a bumpy ride," Chad warned, doing his best Bette Davis imitation.

Janine could only envision *any* ride being smoother than what she'd just been through.

The car moved slowly over the rubble, its riders waiting expectantly and nervously for more aftershocks. Janine was positive one was due the exact moment the car came precariously close to the drop-off as Chad maneuvered them around a large rock that the car couldn't possibly have ridden over. Additional earth-shakes, though, held off. When the next one did come, it—along with the others that followed—was comparatively insignificant.

"I do believe the worst may be over." Chad finally allowed himself that bit of optimism. He flashed Janine a triumphant smile, much like a climber who had just mastered some exceptionally difficult mountain terrain in the company of a heartfelt friend.

For the first, but not the last time, Janine remembered how wonderful it had been pressed so tightly against his hard and muscled body while the hailstorm of rocks had fallen helter-skelter all around them.

♥ *Chapter Four* ♥

DR. ROGER LEWIS LOOKED a little ragged around the edges, and *he was*; he assured himself that *things* could be worse. He dispensed with all superfluous introductions, as regarded the new arrivals. "The facilities were designed to withstand just this sort of event," he said and actually sounded more confident than he looked and was. "That said, people are less ideally designed and, Lou, I'm afraid Jack was...."

"Hurt?" Lou interrupted. The hysterical sound of her concern told anyone who listened—it certainly told Janine and Chad—that Lou's involvement with Dr. Jack Ledben was certainly more serious than Lou was want to let on.

"...sideswiped by a falling bookcase, actually," Roger continued. His accompanying look commanded Lou not to go off the deep end just because of what was actually a minor incident compared to all else Roger had to deal with at the moment. "It's only a scratch. How about the three of you? You look a little battle-weary, to say the very least."

"We were out of the car and clearing the road of debris when the quake hit." Chad was spokesman for the three. "I'm afraid we all got shook up just a bit. Lou has a nasty bump on the back of her head that Hank should take a look at."

"And *you* seem to have developed a slight limp since last I saw you," Roger observed. Very little escaped him.

"A sprain, I think," Chad confessed. "Actually, my shoulder is what's giving me the most trouble."

"Hank is in the dispensary," Roger said. "I want all of you to check in with him. Then, I can use all the help I can to get things straightened out around here. Everything that wasn't bolted down took quite a little ride, and there's been considerable breakage." He had something even more specific in mind for Janine. "Miss Woof, I would especially appreciate it if you'd look in on the kitchen as soon as you feel up to it. We could all use some coffee, and Jenny, the girl in charge, pending your arrival, was one of our casualties."

"Dead?" Lou figured the worst, her face ashen.

"Hardly," Roger assured. "Hysteria. It was her first earthquake, and she happened to be in the restroom at the time. I'm hoping she's settled down a bit by now, but she certainly was none too steady on her feet before and after the outhouse tipped over and before Hank gave her a sedative."

"Come on, Janine." Chad took her arm. "No time like the present to get a clean bill of health and get into the thick of things, as regards your new job."

"Sorry about your introduction to our little place," Roger apologized before Janine got led away. "I'd hoped for you to have a more sedate and mundane hello to the premises."

He smiled ruefully, combing large fingers through his shock of tousled red hair. Someone shouted something about "broken beakers" and some ruined lab experiment.

Janine and Chad lost Lou to Jack Ledben at the dispensary.

Jack wasn't as strikingly handsome as Chad, and he was dark-complexioned where Chad was all sunny blond, but he had decidedly masculine good looks that complemented Lou's feminine attractiveness. He had a bandage over his right eyebrow, another combined wrapping of the index and middle fingers of his right hand.

The line at the dispensary, once long, was nonexistent when the three got there. While Roger had insisted everyone check in, most everyone had been and gone while Janine, Lou, and Chad had been slowly driving the rock-strewn, and periodically shaken, road up the mountainside.

"A little lousy on your timing, aren't you, Janine?" Dr. Hank Heidelburg said in greeting. Having been with the U.S. Geological Society team on Mt. Rainier when Janine had been working summers at the Henry Jackson Fish Hatchery, he remembered how she'd contracted poison ivy one particular summer; Hank had taken full advantage of her *lying-in* to get in some chess with her. "Shall I prescribe bed rest so I can win back some of my losses from Rainier?"

"I suspect that depends upon whether you'd prefer chess to coffee," she said; Hank looked confused. "I'm here to head up the kitchen staff, remember?"

"You wouldn't see if you could run down a few missing butter horns while you're at it, would you?" he asked. "I'm sure there should be some around some-where, but Jenny couldn't find a proverbial pot to ..." He aborted his intended derogatory finale and smiled. "Jenny is such a nice girl, but she does need some su-pervision to get her organized. I think anyone's coffee, after hers, will seem God-sent."

"I hear she took the earthquake hard." Chad scooted to a sitting position atop one of the two ex-amination tables.

"It's nothing from which she isn't going to re-cover. "Earthquakes can be a little unnerving for even us veterans. Why, I remember a quake I went through in Calcutta in...." He apparently thought better of con-tinuing his story at the minute. "I'll tell you both about that when we have more time—and are hopefully all eating butter horns—if I haven't told it to you already. Right now, I suppose, we'd better get on to dealing with *this* quake, or the results thereof. Janine, if you would proceed into the ladies' dressing room, right over there, please." He pointed to a small area cur-tained off from the main room. "Chad, I'll just have you strip down to your skivvies right here and now if you would, please."

"It's my shoulder that's bothering me, doc," Chad argued.

"I doubt your shoulder is giving you that limp you hobbled in here on," Hank argued.

Janine disappeared behind the curtain and won-dered if she were required to strip, too. She decided not. Aside from a few minor scratches and bruises, she'd survived pretty well. Chad had kept her amaz-ingly well protected during the rainfalls of rocks that had skittered down the mountainside.

"Anything indicating magma flows?" Chad asked Hank; Janine's ears perked up.

"Not that I know of," Hank replied and, then, asked Chad to raise his right arm. "Ethan came down from the fumaroles yesterday and said he thought there was an increase in steam from all of the vents on the North Slope. There was so much cloud cover, though, he couldn't be sure. He's up there now with Simmons. They went up as soon as the quake let things quit bouncing a bit. They've radioed back no sign of any blatantly new activity. The old mountain apparently just experienced a more pronounced burp than usual."

Janine had inadvertently left a break in the curtains when she'd entered through them. It wasn't a large crack, but she realized quite suddenly it did give her a good look at Chad who was now minus his shirt, pants, shoes, and socks. Her immediate reaction was to turn away out of respect for Chad's privacy. Her second re-action was to rationalize that it wasn't as if Chad were stark naked. Having been raised in a household of boys, Janine knew everything there was to know about the anatomical differences between the sexes. She'd certainly seen her brothers, and lots of other men, in swimming suits. Chad's Jockey bikini briefs were ad-mittedly skimpier than some bathing trunks, but they were certainly sufficient so that Janine needn't feel guilty when shifting to get an even better look.

She examined his physique for flaws. It was in-conceivable that a man so attractive *in* clothes could be equally attractive, or more so, when most of his clothes were off. If there was anything physically wrong with Chad's body, though, Janine couldn't see it.

He had the smoothly chiseled musculature of those gymnasts she'd sometimes seen shirtless in the WSU gymnastics room. Either his chest was hairless from his neck to his slightly indented navel, or the hair he did have there was too fine and blond to be noticeable. His arms were molded with muscle, and his legs looked straight off some classical Greco-Roman sculpture in a museum. In fact, his whole body seemed to be one that Praxiteles would have jumped at the opportunity of carving from marble in that sculptor's heyday of doing Greek art.

"Nothing too horribly wrong with your shoulder that I can see," Hank diagnosed for Chad. "Although if it continues to give you problems, stop by in a couple of days, and we'll give you some pain killer or another more extensive look-see. Same goes for your leg. I'd tell you to stay off the leg, but I know just how far you'd go toward following that good bit of advice, so I'm assuming it'll mend in time if you just don't go out of your way to use and abuse it. You'll have some nasty bruises along your back and along the backs of your legs—"

"Ouch!" Chad responded when Hank touched a particularly nasty and tender bruise.

"—but there is nothing to do for those but let them look as bad as they please before they go away. Now, get dressed and go make yourself useful."

"Janine?" Chad asked.

Embarrassed by what she assumed was his discovery that she was observing through the crack in the curtain, she blushed a deep scarlet and turned away. Chad's query, though, had nothing to do with her playing Peeping-Jill.

"I'll see that she finds her way to the kitchen," Hank promised. "Or, if I find anything seriously wrong with her, I'll send you word. Confidentially, she looks in far better shape than you do. The next quake, I recommend that you follow her lead."

"Right!" Chad replied; Janine noticed how he modestly didn't boast that he was in his present condition, Janine in her present condition, only because he had acted as a human shield between her and rainstorms of stones.

Hank joined Janine in her curtained cubicle. He verified what they both suspected; she was in A-1 shape, considering everything. She vaguely remembered a blow to the back of her head, but it must have been a glancing one, because it hadn't broken the skin or even left a detectable bump.

Hank gave her directions to the kitchen and told her she'd probably find Brad Wayne waiting there for her. "Brad's the token college jock hired on to do the heavy work in the kitchen area. Please don't, like Jenny did, count upon him being of much help in preparing menus or meals."

He turned his attention to Lou who showed up as Janine was on her way out. "And, where have you been hiding with this goose egg of yours?" he asked her, his fingers probing her chestnut-colored hair at the back of her head. She'd been less lucky than Janine. "Are you seeing double, by any chance?"

Janine stopped, but Hank hadn't completely shifted all of his attention from her to Lou. "You, young lady," he told Janine, "can do everyone the most good by getting to the kitchen, fast, and getting it operational. There's nothing more demoralizing to any group than having its food come out less than mouth-watering—which is what it has been doing for these past couple of weeks. Though, bless Jenny, even Brad, they did give it the old college try."

"I'll be fine, Janine," Lou assured.

"Oh, became a doctor of medicine, did you, on your wild ride up the mountain?" Hank mocked. "You just let *me* decide whether you'll be okay or not."

Lou looked duly chastised, in a good-natured sort of way, and Janine headed for the kitchen.

"You want coffee, we've got someone coming to make it," said the young man with the build of a weight-lifter when Janet poked her head into the kitchen.

Brad was in the middle of the floor, trying his flour-covered best to sort scattered pots and pans that had been obviously dented in their recent unruly descent from their hangers along the walls. He hadn't looked up, apparently having merely sensed Janine's presence.

"I do believe I *am* the scheduled coffee-maker," Janine said with a smile.

"Really?" He turned his head in her direction and scrambled to his feet. He brushed off a pair of fringed jean cut-offs that revealed his highly muscled legs to good advantage. His equally flour-dusted T-shirt, complete with its WSU logo, sprouted his large neck and a pair of well-developed arms. "Everybody has been in here looking for coffee and something to eat, and I never could figure out how the coffee pot works."

"I think one WSU alumni and one WSU student can handle the problems here, don't you? I'm Janine Woof, by the way."

"We've been eagerly awaiting your arrival, Janine Woof. And I do mean *eagerly.*"

"You're Brad, right?"

"Right."

"So, can you at least point me in the direction of this coffee machine, Brad?"

It was one of the multi-pot percolator affairs found mainly in restaurants. It was very simple to operate if you knew the procedure. It was very frustrating, though—poor Brad!—if you hadn't a notion of what you were doing.

Janine quickly got the coffee brewing and found Hank's requested butter horns in the walk-in freezer next to the butter beans. *Not* with the bread, where she would have expected. Every head of every kitchen had his or her own system that worked best, and Janine suspected her predecessor's was going to take a little revising before Janine was comfortable with it.

She spread the rolls out on large trays after generously slathering the top of each roll with butter. She slid the trays in an oven kept operational, like everything else at the camp, by the generator that had been brought in for just such emergencies. As soon as the rolls and coffee were ready, she had all intentions of loading up a platter of rolls and sending Brad around the camp with it. As it turned out, though, the smell of brewing java and baking butter-soaked sweet rolls brought everyone to her. There was a line-up well before either coffee or rolls were ready.

Roger arrived soon after serving began in earnest, as drawn by the luscious scents as was everyone else. "Don't ever let anyone tell you *every* woman can cook," he told Janine, savoring his latest bite of butter horn as if she'd made it from scratch.

"Amen," Hank agreed from across the room. He'd been one of the first to the kitchen when the rolls came out of the oven. After sending Janine in search of them, he'd obviously not been about to let everyone else reap the benefits of his efforts without him.

"Of course, Jenny was hired to *assist* in the kitchen, not take charge of it," Roger added, "so it's not fair to criticize her. She did the best she could in a pinch, and none of us have turned into walking skeletons because of it, but...." He shook his head, leaving it at that.

"How *is* Jenny?" Janine asked. She had to smile at Brad who was attacking two large rolls and a large glass of milk at a nearby table; he'd obviously forgotten that butter-soaked sugar-filled sweet rolls were hardly standard diet for any aspiring college athlete in training.

"Jenny will be just fine, come morning," Hank predicted, having overheard Janine's question to Roger. The room really wasn't at all large, having to house only the twenty-plus people associated with the project, at any one sitting. "All we have to do is convince her she's already been through the worst. I mean, after a bear and an earthquake, what else is there?"

"Another thousand or so feet could blow off the mountain and take us all with it, for one," Jack Ledben joked, arriving from the dispensary where he'd left

Lou under enforced bed rest until Hank could determine whether her double vision was going to go away or heralded something more serious.

"Let poor Jenny hear that, and that'll be the last we'll see of her," Hank warned.

"Nah!" Brad begged to differ. "She needs the money for college, or she would have been out of here like a shot when the bear almost took off Barry's arm. Where's she going to find another good-paying job like this one so far into the season?"

"Nevertheless, I think we must avoid all mention of possible eruption around Jenny, shouldn't we?" Hank seriously suggested. "We wouldn't want you having to pick up the slack of one less helper in Janine's kitchen, now, would we?"

"No, we jolly well would not!" Brad agreed.

Chad came in, looking more than a little run-ragged. The sun was coming up outside, and he'd really had very little rest, except for the catnap he'd caught in the early stages of the drive up. Janine had put aside a couple of hot rolls to make sure he got some, no matter what time he came trailing in. She excused herself from Roger's table, where she' been taking a break, and joined Chad at the back of the room.

"Tell me I'm too late for even the leftovers, and I'll show you a quick suicide," he said, his wide smile doing a lot to alleviate the tiredness that had managed to creep into his face.

"Come on, now," Janine chided, "do you really think I'd feed the masses and leave the prince standing hungry on the sidelines?"

"A maid of true mercy," he whispered and his smile widened. He followed her to the counter, and she retrieved the promised rolls from the warmer. She put them and a fresh cup of coffee on his tray.

"Could I exchange the coffee for cold milk, or is that looking a gift horse in the mouth?"

"Are you and Brad both in training?" She reached for a clean and unbroken glass from the arrangement Brad had made, earlier, on a nearby counter top.

"Since when does training include wolfing down butter horns?" Chad asked, evidently deducing from the crumbs left on Brad's tray—there was certainly no other incriminating evidence remaining—that the young athlete had been off diet at least for the morning.

Janine filled the glass with milk by raising the large chrome ball of the dispenser.

Chad drained half the glass and eyed Janine over the rim of it.

"Fine pick-me-up, now what's for breakfast?" Hank called, dramatically licking each of the five fingers of his right hand.

"Please, don't aggravate the cook," Roger commanded. "I've already let her know that, after our two weeks of something far less than Julia-Childs cuisine, she has us at a decided disadvantage."

"So, we'll call this breakfast and let her get settled in," Hank conceded graciously.

"Actually, I was thinking more along the lines of pancakes about, oh…." Janine checked her wristwatch which had miraculously survived the quake. "…seven?"

She was surprised by the spontaneous cheer from the group in residence.

"You are truly a godsend, my dear." Chad leaned to give her a kiss on the cheek.

The group cheered again—even louder—and Janine blushed as red as the canned beets on the shelves behind her. This brought much clapping of hands.

HEART ON FIRE, BY WILLIAM MALTESE

♥ *Chapter Five* ♥

JANINE TOLD HERSELF that the only thing behind her whirlwind activities in the kitchen was her sense of job and doing that job as well as competently possible. However, in the back of her mind, through all the preparations of breakfast and getting it out of the way, her mind kept helplessly replaying the simple and harmless kiss Chad had placed on her cheek to the applause and cheers of all onlookers. No matter how often she reminded herself that it was a spontaneous kiss—probably as chaste as any brother pecking the cheek of a sister—she couldn't quite shake the special way she'd felt when his lips had touched her. She'd kissed other men full on the lips and not derived anywhere nearly a similar sensation of pleasure.

She conducted a less-than-thorough survey of the immediate food supply and set Brad to work on a more comprehensive tallying of what was available while she roughed out menus for the next couple of days. She decided on *shit-on-a-shingle* (AKA chipped beef on toast) for lunch later that day, because SOS was simple. Besides which, what with pre-dawn coffee and sweet rolls, followed by pancakes and home-made

51

sugar syrup at seven, she figured she'd get few complaints—if any. Her decision to have a simple stew for supper took care of scheduling the day, and she spent the next few minutes putting on the beef to boil and gather up the necessary vegetables for peeling. She could have called Brad to help, but she welcomed her chores with the same enthusiasm with which she'd welcomed all her self-assigned busy-work since Chad had kissed her earlier that morning.

For not the first time, or last, she consciously thrust the kissing incident to the back of her mind, marveling instead at how she seemed so fresh and vitalized, considering all she'd been through. If anything, she should be dead on her feet from lack of sleep. She suspected she wouldn't have to do more than let her head hit the pillow that evening before she would be off in Dreamland. She would welcome that. Going over and over Chad's kiss, as harmless as it admittedly was, wasn't something she would relish doing alone in the darkness of her sleeping quarters.

"Time for you to have a break, isn't it?" Chad asked from the door. He was with a tall brown-haired man, with brown eyes, who looked attractive in a kind of gangling sort of way. The man was wearing a khaki-green shirt, fatigue pants and combat boots. Janine couldn't recall having seen him before. "You shouldn't make the mistake of being too perfect at the beginning," Chad warned her, coming farther into the room and drawing the other man along in his wake, "or we'll too quickly forget that you rescued us from Jenny and Brad's culinary disasters. Keep us appreciative as long as you can."

"I'm in the process of preparing SOS for lunch," Janine said. "Stew for supper. Think those are pedestrian enough for starters?"

"I like SOS," the tall man said and followed Chad's example to sit opposite Janine at the dining-room table she was using as a supplemental work area.

"That from the mouth of someone probably subjected to more chipped beef on toast than anyone else you'll find here," Chad said and gave Janine a broad wink. He had such sexy eyes. He had such a sexy mouth, it…. "Ethan George, Janine Woof," Chad interrupted her train of thought, and she thanked him for it. "Ethan is our resident pilot. He got a lot of expertise flying military missions in Afghanistan. Pull out that map of yours, Ethan, and show Janine the whereabouts of Troutdale as the crow or your plane flies."

On their drive in, before the earthquake had made small-talk impossible, Janine had mentioned to Chad, in passing, that there was an old friend of her great-grandmother in Troutdale that Janine had promised she'd *try* to drop by to see; the woman in question getting up in years. Janine had since forgotten having mentioned any of that and was surprised Chad had remembered.

To take her mind off any additional thoughts of Chad, she concentrated on Ethan. She'd heard that a lot of veterans came back ill-adjusted to civilian life. Every so often, she heard of another one who went off the deep end. She searched Ethan's brown eyes for some sign of pent-up madness waiting (like Mt. St. Helens?) to explode. His were two of the saddest eyes she'd ever seen, and she realized she'd had that impression—unformulated until then—from the very start.

"Troutdale is here," Ethan said, his long but graceful index finger pinpointing a spot on the map he'd unfolded on the table in front of them. Janine got up and came around for a look that put the topography into better perspective."

"And we're...?" she asked.

"Here," Chad obliged, his finger stabbing a spot not all that far from where Ethan's fingertip still rested. However, Janine was familiar enough with maps to know that distances could be deceiving, especially when a person didn't have wings. If the two spots on the map were within a few inches of one another, the only connecting roadway was one via the little town of Cougar. That was a long way, even longer when considering the likely conditions of the road after the recent earthquake.

"No way but through Cougar?" Janine asked.

She knew she had promised to look in on Sarah Zent, but she wouldn't be sorry if there was some excuse why the visit wasn't possible.

"How about if I walk cross-country?" she suggested and hoped she sounded interested, if just because Chad had gone to such bother.

"A system of gorges, gullies, and natural indentations run this way." Ethan's finger slid back and forth along a position that separated the camp from Troutdale. "It'd take you longer to walk the distance than it would to drive there via Cougar, even if you were in tip-top physical condition." He seemed to insinuate (and probably rightly so) that he knew tip-top physical condition and didn't see her with it. So much for

Janine's self-boasting that she was capable of successfully heading off across wilderness terrain.

"So, I tell Great-Grandmother Woof that I at least made the effort," Janine said, speaking her thoughts aloud.

"And if Great-Grandma Woof asks why you didn't have sense enough to fly?" Chad asked.

"Great-Grandma may be old, but she's nowhere nearly senile enough to think her great-granddaughter has wings," Janine reminded.

"What if you and I can persuade Ethan, here, to take you over to Troutdale in the copter?" Chad clarified.

"I don't think Roger is going to approve of the team copter and the project pilot being utilized to taxi me back and forth to socialize." She wasn't about to get on the bad side of her boss by doing something not even she was all that certain she even wanted to do.

"How can Roger complain when Troutdale is on the way?" Chad wanted to know.

"On the way to where?" Janine asked suspiciously.

"On the way to several experiments I have on the North Slope. There are all sorts of geodimeters, tiltmeters, and seismometers that have to be monitored on a regular basis in the Troutdale vicinity. So, why can't they be read while you're visiting an old-old-old family friend?

"I wouldn't want anyone thinking I was being given preferential treatment," Janine said.

"Who's going to complain after you've saved us from more of Jenny and Brad's cooking?"

"You thought the earthquake was bad," Ethan said, and his grin looked as if it were exploring unfamiliar facial territory; he didn't remind Janine of someone who smiled all that often, "Wait until you see the one that would result if Jenny and Brad ever got back to doing whatever it was they were doing in the kitchen before you arrived to save us all. I was in the service for two years, and no military cook would have ever dared serve up the stuff those two did."

"Ethan doesn't lie, so help me God," Chad said and crossed his heart with one hand. "You keep on delivering decent meals on time, and you can pretty much write your own ticket around here, even as regards gratis helicopter rides."

"Maybe if I can clear it with Roger," Janine conceded. If the opportunity was there, she owed it to her great-grandmother to take advantage of it, whether Janine was enthused or not. She'd probably feel guilty as hell is she could have gone, didn't, and Sarah Zent dropped dead before she could convey Great-Grandma Woof's hellos.

Besides, Janine meeting Sarah Zent just might prove a nice diversion from cooking 24/7.

"I'll clear it with Roger," Chad volunteered. "You just keep rolling the good food off the assembly line in the meantime."

Ethan refolded the map, tucked it into his shirt pocket and asked, little-boy polite, to be excused. Before he left, Janine asked him if he wanted something to eat, positive she'd not seen him at either the pre-dawn coffee and sweet rolls, or later at breakfast. If all the team were as thin as Ethan, Janine would have genuinely believed Jenny and Brad's cooking had been totally indigestible.

"Thanks, but I stuffed on candy during this morning's flight."

"He was up in the copter, checking the mountain, while we were digging out down here," Chad explained.

"I think I can hold off until lunch," Ethan assured, "especially since, as I said, I actually like SOS."

Chad sat back in his chair, reflectively watching Ethan's exit. Janine looked at all the unpeeled vegetables she had on the table in front of her. They were a good excuse to ask Chad to go. In the back of her mind, though, she knew she had plenty of time. More time if she enlisted Brad's efforts as a peeler. There was something about being with Chad that she thoroughly enjoyed.

"Ethan is a really nice guy," Chad said, something in his voice insinuating the need for Janine to question his definition of *nice*.

"He certainly *seemed* that," she said.

"There's a surprisingly large amount of strength inside that skinny body of his. I mean, he may look like the next wind storm is going to blow him over, but I guess he had some pretty impressive kills during his time in the military. Not that he'd ever admit to it."

"He seemed calm enough." There had been something about him, though, similar to a too-tightly coiled spring, that Janine thought she might not like to see come suddenly unwound.

"I guess his best friend in Afghanistan got blown away," Chad said. "He's never gone into specifics, and I've never had the guts to press him about it."

Janine felt pretty lucky she'd been as little affected by all of the wars of the world as she might have been, especially considering she had six brothers. Glen had even served in the Army but had never ended up anywhere dangerous. He'd been in Korea but only long *after* the Korean War (or Conflict, or whatever). He'd finished up his enlistment at a Portland, Oregon, enlistment and examination station. Her brother Johnny had been in and out of the Navy, between wars, married and had three kids. Bob had been discharged from the Army, had married Stella, a little Bobby on the way before U.S. troops started being seriously shipped to the Middle East. Brewster had somehow finagled a deferment by some hook or crook (just prior to his marriage to wife one) that still wasn't considered a subject for polite family conversation. Carl and Darrel had gotten college deferments; Carl had been closest to going but had ended up spending all of his time at Fort Ord, California.

Only cousin Granger, the son of Uncle Tal and Wendy, on Janine's mother's side of the family, had been killed on duty (in Iraq). Another cousin, again on Janine's mother's side, had been wounded, but Janine hadn't known him very well. Even in families as close as hers, it was difficult to be all that close to everyone. Cliques and friendships, some stronger than others, were always forming and breaking down.

"A penny for your thoughts." Chad brought her out of her reverie. As trite as his interruption might have been, it seemed charming. Even in the light from the industrial neon tubes overhead, the look in his eyes was purely magical.

"I was thinking about how wars affect so many lives," she said.

He fished into the watch pocket of his jeans (did anyone ever put a watch there, anymore?), and retrieved a penny which he placed on the table. She took the coin and found it still sensuously warm from his body.

"A lot of Woofs and Farnwells die in wars?" he asked and reached for a small carrot which he began to eat. He had even, white teeth.

"Surprisingly, no," Janine admitted, "especially considering how many of them *could* have ended up dead."

There was the distracting sound of the walk-in freezer door swinging open. Brad emerged with steaming breath and clapping his gloved hands to warm them.

"Ink in my pen froze up." He pushed the door closed behind him. "That's for sure a job that requires a pencil." He pulled his inventory clipboard from underneath one arm and dropped it on a nearby counter.

"I'll help you with that later, Brad, if you help me peel these vegetables, now, for evening stew," Janine promised. She was giving Chad his cue to leave, and he took it gracefully, promising to see them both later.

When he was gone, Janine immediately missed him and wished he were back.

She looked up to realize Brad was smiling at her from across the table. Somehow, he had not only inserted himself into the spot just vacated by Chad, but he had already peeled several potatoes and deposited them in the pan next to his right elbow. The way Janine's kitchen activity had come to a mysterious stop upon Chad's departure hadn't gone unnoticed by Brad.

"Like him, do you?" Brad intuited.

"Who?" Janine replied innocently, knowing she was beginning to blush despite all efforts not to. "Oh, you mean, Chad?"

"Did you see anyone else just here, chatting up our head cook?"

"Actually, he stopped by to tell me he thought he might be able to arrange transportation for me to visit a family friend in Troutdale."

"Right." Brad didn't sound as if he believed her.

♥ *Chapter Six* ♥

"BUSY?" CHAD ASKED, appearing tired but nonetheless handsome.

Janine certainly *looked* busy, having just made pie-crust dough for the bacon quiches she had scheduled for the next morning. She was as covered with flour as Brad had been when she'd spotted him earlier sorting dented pots and pans on the recently earthquaked kitchen floor.

"I thought we could both break for a walk," Chad suggested.

She checked her wristwatch after first having to wipe its crystal clear of flour. It was almost ten o'clock at night. She hadn't realized it was so late.

"Brad!" she called to the young athlete moving through the rows of restacked canned goods with his clipboard and pencil in hand. "Why don't you call it a night, since we both have to get up with the chickens tomorrow?"

"Right!" He appeared from between the tins of green and lima beans. He spotted Chad and flashed a wide *well what do we have here* grin. "Hi, Chad! Long time no see. I thought for sure you'd be in bed by now."

"I don't have to get up nearly as early as the two of you," Chad reminded. He and Janine watched while Brad performed a none-too-hurried exit.

"He thinks we have something going on between us," Janine said lightly. Her voice seemed to come out downright strange whenever she was with Chad.

"We *do* have something going on between us. A proposed walk. Right?"

"It's a bit late for strolling bear-infested forest, isn't it? It might be smarter if the two of us skipped the walk and went to bed."

Immediately, she realized how *that* came out sounding. Nor was the usually gentlemanly Chad gentlemanly enough to let it pass. "Shouldn't we at least go out on a date first?"

"You know *exactly* what I meant." Janine blushed. She'd done an awfully lot of blushing since first meeting Chad.

"Damn, and I was just about to accept your invitation to bed, no questions asked."

Janine blushed deeper and was furious at the telltale redness she just knew was obvious as hell even through her dark complexion and her summer tan. She couldn't imagine why a few words from Chad continually converted her into a giddy schoolgirl. It wasn't as if she hadn't had a lot of practice deflecting passes from men more aggressive than Chad, because she had. She'd gone to WSU where she'd come across more than her fair share of wannabe Don Juans who weren't at all shy about letting their intentions be known. She'd successfully fended them off, without turning all beet red, each step of the way. She wasn't at all pleased that she seemed unable to exert the same control around Chad.

"It is such a beautiful night outside," Chad enticed. "The majority of the dust has settled, but there's still enough of it in the air to make the moon look rusty-red. Nothing like a bit of night air, either, to make you really fall asleep once your head hits the pillow."

"I doubt either of us will have trouble sleeping tonight," she prophesied.

"Is that a *no,* then?" He sounded genuinely disappointed.

If nothing else, he was persuasive.

She did like his company. She was flattered to be asked by him out into the moonlight. Of all the men on this project, Chad was by far the most handsome. A leisurely walk, with him, at close of day, *did* sound inviting. So what if a bear had almost taken an arm off the previous cook only a couple of weeks before? If that bear had been hunted down and killed by park rangers (which it had), that didn't mean it didn't have a brother, sister, mother, father, uncle or aunt, or cousins, out there somewhere, ready to take revenge on these two-legged interlopers into bear territory.

"Bears?" She thought that as good an argument as any against walking the night.

"I'll protect you, promise."

"With your bum leg or with your bum arm?" She smiled wryly.

"Any bear would eat slow-mo me, you getting away Scot-free."

"Mmmmmmmm."

"You really don't think I'm asking you out to take advantage of you behind some pine tree, do you?"

There were some men she was suspicious of from the minute they entered a room. Chad wasn't one of them.

"On the other hand," he continued, "if you're genuinely not up to walking because you're just dead tired...."

Okay, she *was* tempted by Chad, by the supposedly rusty-red moonlight, and by walking in the presence of both.

There was no sense denying that she was attracted to Chad. She'd liked his looks even before she'd seen him stripped to his Jockey shorts and putting his until-then hidden physical perfection on naked display. Not that it was *just* his handsome face and marvelous body that attracted her. After all, he wasn't the only handsome hunk to whom she'd been exposed in her lifetime. However, he did come off one of the few who seemed to hold out promise of something more to offer a woman besides *just* an attractive *façade*. Trying to define that *something more* was something else again.

"Okay, I'd love to take a walk with you," she conceded.

"Good."

Janine gave a final check of the dough in the refrigerator. Since it was obvious it hadn't gone anywhere since she'd put it in there, she suspected she was merely indulging another stall. Assured the dough was in place, she decided *any* reason for dragging her feet was foolish. He'd only asked her for a walk, not proposed marriage. She was too busy making more of the harmless invitation than was really there. She had only known Chad for a few short hours and vice versa. Nothing happened between two people in that short of time, no matter what the romance books said to the contrary.

"Think I'll need a sweater?" She switched off the kitchen lights behind them. Suddenly, she was standing in shadow with him. It was likely even darker outside, and....

"I doubt you'll need a sweater."

Mention of her sweater, though, did remind her that she still had unpacking to do. Chad had earlier carried her bags to the room Janine would be sharing with Lou, but Janine hadn't even yet seen the room; she hoped she could find it when the time came. Lou wouldn't have unpacked for her, either, because Lou was still in the dispensary under Hank's care. By rights, Janine should be in the dispensary, checking up on the well-being of her friend, instead of off on a moonlight stroll. Except, it was late and, even if Lou weren't asleep, Hank wasn't likely to look too kindly on Janine disturbing him or his patient.

It was downright balmy outside even with Janine having spent most of her day in an overheated kitchen.

"Nice," she confessed, aware of the way the moonlight, definitely rusty-red, enhanced Chad's good looks and the landscape. The light caught in his tousled blond hair and held there. He looked like a Botticelli angel slightly too close to hellish flames.

"That way is the easiest slope to climb." He pointed to their left. "There's, also, a pretty good view of the valley from there."

They started off, side by side, but not touching.

"Hard to imagine there's now such a drastic difference between this side of the mountain and the other, isn't it?" He pulled back the branch of a low-growing pine so it wouldn't whip Janine's face on her way by.

The May 1980 explosion had devastated 200 square miles when the North Face had bulged and then exploded. Trees still stood here but, up and over the mountain, similar timberland had been toppled like matchsticks. Plant and animal life still thrived here but, up and over the mountain, similar wildlife had been burned to a crisp before and after being suffocated by hot dust and gases, as well as buried beneath huge avalanches of viscous mud. The team camp was erected on the South Slope because volcanic activity continued to be seemingly centered on the other side.

Like everyone, Janine had seen the newspaper photos and TV coverage of the May 1980 blow. A jet flight from Seattle to Spokane had shown her a distance-distorted view of the blasted side of the mountain, but it was still hard for her to grasp just how much damage had been done is so short a time. Here, it seemed so deceptively blissful, nothing insinuating they walked atop a potential powder keg that had already gone off with one big bang, no guarantees that it wouldn't go off again, taking all of this and them with it. It made Janine acutely aware of her mortality.

"You'd never know there'd been an earthquake this morning." She allowed Chad to help her over a step-way of rock on the trail.

His hand was sensuously rough with calluses against her decidedly softer palm. Working at Marine World, unlike working in the field, hadn't found her frequently scrambling over volcanic barriers to test for aquatic life in super-heated stream remains.

She freed her hand, albeit reluctantly, from his.

"It's not much farther to the view," he promised.

Janine realized she was actually short of breath. It had really been way too long since she'd gotten out and given herself the physical exercise she needed to stay in shape. It was becoming increasingly doubtful that Chad would appreciate *her* body, stripped down, as much as she'd appreciated her peek at his well-toned perfection.

"Here we are." He helped her up on an exposed lip of basalt that proclaimed the mountain's violent construction, even on this benign side of the boiling cauldron.

He sat down and patted a place beside him.

Janine joined him.

"I really must get more exercise," she promised, more for her hearing than for his.

The footpath shouldn't have been nearly as demanding. There was a time she could have taken it on like a mountain goat took on steep crags. Now, she merely found herself envious that Chad wasn't even breathing a little heavily, despite his still-evident limp.

"Maybe it's the view that's taken your breath away," he gave her a suitable alternative.

His cheeks dimpled in the flattering moonlight. His hair continued to look like it held the vestiges of a fire-reflecting halo. His eyes were more gold than gold. How many Biblical saints had been tempted by just such wondrously perfect visions and succumbed to them?

Janine shook her head to clear it. She really should have gone straight to bed, what with the silliness of her suddenly equating herself with Biblical saints, when the only saint around here was the Mt. *Saint* Helens they were sitting on.

Quite suddenly, she realized she was so occupied with Chad's handsomeness that the view provided by Mother Nature had completely escaped her. Consciously, she made an effort to concentrate on what was laid out before her.

"That's Cougar, over there." Chad pointed to flickering pinpoints of light in the distant southwest. "I suspect Troutdale is somewhere through there." He moved his arm slightly east. "Probably not visible because of the trees."

Immediately behind them, the buildings of the camp were mainly dark, a light here and there signifying that a few others might still be up and about.

When Janine felt Chad's arm suddenly around her, like a comforting warm blanket, she turned—like a robot—to meet his lips with hers.

None too quickly, she pulled away, embarrassed for letting things go so far so fast with a man she hardly knew. She was even more embarrassed in knowing that she had shamelessly enjoyed each and every second of it.

"Now, you're sorry you let that happen." Chad was stating fact, not asking a question.

"Nonsense," she denied, although he'd read her mind—for not the first time, either.

It would have been downright ridiculous to accuse him of taking unfair advantage. Janine wasn't some silly ninny straight out of grade school who'd never been French kissed.

"I do, however, think we should get back," she appended. She needed to mull over the kissed-him, kissed-her consequences of her simultaneous exposure to wondrous moonlight and a wondrous Dr. Chad Samuels.

They got up and headed back.

She maneuvered the natural rock stairway, this time, on her own, without accepting the offer of his helpful hand.

When he stopped suddenly, she stopped with him. Hers was a purely reflexive response, an automation instigated by being so in sync with him and his movements.

"Well, I'm *not* sorry I kissed you," he said. "I've wanted to kiss you from the first moment I saw you, and that peck on the cheek I managed to steal over that glass of milk and hot rolls only made me more determined to sample the real thing."

"So, for the moment, let's just leave it at that, yes?" she suggested. "We'll have more of our wits about us after a night's rest, and we can move on from there."

Snake or bear lurking in the shadows, she left Chad standing where he was. Her heart was beating so hard and so fast that, when she finally reached her and Lou's room, she was thankful Lou wasn't there to ask what the loud and speedy drum-beat was all about.

Janine didn't even try to tell herself that something hadn't definitely changed in her life, although she wasn't yet prepared to put any engraved-in-steel definition as to what that certain *something* actually was.

HEART ON FIRE, BY WILLIAM MALTESE

♥ *Chapter Seven* ♥

"LOU!" JANINE EXCLAIMED, looking up from the chocolate-chip cookies that had come out less satisfactory than she'd been hoping. She suspected the problem was to do with stale shortening; she should have opened a new can.

"Smells good," her friend said and came deeper into the room. She weaved through the tables until she reached the one closest to Janine behind the counter. She laid her notebook on the table and sat down.

Janine joined her. The last pan of cookies had come out five minutes ago and, less-than-perfect or not, would have to do. They'd probably be hardened into bricks—the likes of which had built many a real tollhouse (thus, their name?)—but that would take until morning. By today's lunch, they'd still be edible. With a group that hadn't had dessert all that often, over the last two weeks, the cookies would undoubtedly disappear before their to-brick-status conversions.

"Still having double vision?" Janine sat across from her friend.

"Comes and goes; mostly goes. Hank predicts it'll be completely cleared in a couple more days, and I can get back into the full swing of things, then."

Janine felt guilty for not having dropped by the dispensary as often as she'd intended.

"So?" Lou asked. "Is this a good time for you, between breakfast and lunch, or should I drop by later?"

"Everything is well in hand." Janine knew Lou's timing couldn't have been better. Jenny had showed up bright and early that morning with Brad, obviously embarrassed that her earthquake-provoked hysteria had seen the doctor keep her tranquilized for over twenty-four hours. If Jenny was the horrible cook people accused her of being, she was competent enough on the jobs Janine had assigned her; breakfast had proceeded far smoother than if *just* Janine and Brad had managed it.

Janine had seen Chad at breakfast, but she'd successfully avoided any eye contact.

"We're having sauerkraut and wieners for lunch." Janine settled in. "Jenny and Brad have everything in control."

"So," Lou said with an emphasizing sigh in final punctuation. Her bed rest had done her a world of good. She looked fresh and cheerful. Her chestnut-colored hair was fluffy but not flyaway from its morning wash. Her hazel eyes betrayed none of the complications that could still twin Janine, and anything else, on short notice. "Do you want to go over this first...." She tapped the notebook on the table. "...or shall we have you lead off by giving me the behind-the-scenes royal tour of the kitchen?"

Janine couldn't imagine why Lou would want to see more of the kitchen than she already could see from out front.

Lou eyed Janine curiously. "These, my dear," she said and tapped the notebook, "are my notes from the experiments I've ongoing on the North Face. Are we carrying on the same conversation, or did my knock on the head do more than double my vision?"

Janine was confused and looked it.

"Let me guess," Lou said. "Roger hasn't talked to you, yet, this morning?"

As if conjured by incantation, Roger picked that particular moment to make his appearance. "Ah!" he greeted from the kitchen doorway.

"A little late, aren't we, Roger?" Lou scolded. "I've arrived with my notes, and Janine is wondering what possible interest I could have in sauerkraut and wienies, besides eating them."

"I'm afraid I got tied up looking at the readouts Simmons pulled out of the crater this morning," Roger apologized and joined them.

"Increased dome buildup, the way I hear it," Lou commented knowledgeably.

"Definitely, but with no corresponding visible magma extrusions," Roger confirmed. "You know the pattern. Same-o, same-o. Ho-hum, earthquake or no."

As far as research on volcanic activity had progressed in the last hundred years, everyone at the table knew there were still unknown nuances to be explored. The intensity of the May 1980 eruption of Mt. St. Helens had taken *everyone* by surprise—even with all the scientific paraphernalia monitoring the mountain at the time.

"Anyway, have you two talked over the temporary exchange?" Roger asked the two of them.

"What *exchange?*" Janine's response made it obvious that Lou and she had discussed nothing of the sort.

"It'll only be for a couple of days," Lou promised. "Actually, after…." She lowered her voice to a whisper that wouldn't carry to Jenny and Brad who were busy in the space behind the counter. "…Jenny and Brad's disastrous turn at the culinary helm, I doubt anyone around here will willingly leave me in charge for longer than two days. It'll soon enough become evident that either of the two kids is actually a better cook than I am. Roger is merely intent upon presenting the temporary illusion that we're not really regressing as far as the kitchen is concerned."

"Let's move back and pick this up from the beginning, shall we?" Roger suggested.

"Yes, please." Janine remained confused.

"Lou has some experiments on the North Face that need monitoring," Roger said, "but Hank would rather his patient, one Lou, stay put for a couple more days, until Hank is sure everything is okay in that beautiful Lou-Lou head. We know you hired on as head of kitchen, but we also know that you're a qualified biologist, and Chad suggested…."

"*Chad* suggested," Janine echoed. She hadn't slept at all well after their walk (and kiss) last night. If the night air was supposed to have made her sleepy, she'd managed only tossing and turning into the wee hours.

"Initially, Chad volunteered to make the readings himself," Lou confessed, "but he has his own stuff to look after. His taking on mine, too, might prove a bit much, even for him. I mean, I'm not saying he isn't competent enough to get his *and* my work right, but why take the chance, especially with you here?"

"Besides which, what with the recent increased pressure buildups, earthquakes, and the like," Roger added, "we'd all feel a lot safer if Chad weren't exposed on the North Face any longer than necessary."

"Not that we're willing to stick you bull's-eye in the danger zone," Lou was quick to assure. "You know I wouldn't volunteer you for anything that I thought was really dangerous."

Chad, though, was the one who'd volunteered Janine's services, wasn't he?

"We have no reason to expect any immediate violent activity," Roger assured, "but there's always that unknown quantity whenever dealing with a mountain like this one."

"Chad wouldn't have suggested you substitute, either, if *he* thought there was any danger," Lou said. "You know that."

It wasn't the danger offered by Mt. St. Helens that had Janine worried at the moment. She would be on the North Face *with Chad.* Chad—especially after she'd so easily succumbed to his kiss the night before—was her more immediate concern.

Granted, the two of them would be *working.* Granted, it was only for a *couple* of days. What could possibly happen in two short days—a mere forty-eight hours?

On the other hand, look at what *had* happened in so little time. There'd been an earthquake, during which Janine had been less aware of the earth shaking than of Chad's hard body against her. There'd been a peck on the cheek over sweet rolls and cold milk. There'd been a walk in the dark. There'd been that real, genuine *no mistaking it for anything other than it was* kiss.

"Two days, you say?" Janine asked.

"The readouts could wait, but it would be better for the continuity of the experiments if they were recorded in a timely manner," Lou said, sounding every inch the concerned scientist.

"We hope you can schedule two days of easy meals that Lou, Jenny, and Brad can manage without ruining them and our stomachs completely," Roger said.

"Do they make meals that uncomplicated, I wonder?" Lou joked.

"If they don't, we just might have to surrender experiment results for Janine and decent meals." Roger sounded serious enough to make Janine wonder if he wasn't. "What do we gain by timely experiment data if we perish by bad cooking?"

Lou and Janine laughed, but not even the humor covered the admitted anticipation Janine experienced at the prospect of being even more closely thrown together with Chad.

Roger sniffed the air. "Are those cookies I've been smelling?"

Janine nodded.

"Love cookies," said Roger.

"Everyone loves anything around here after two weeks of Jenny and Brad" Lou was certain.

"Well, what do you say, Janine?" Roger accepted the chocolate-chip cookie she offered. "Think you can cover for Lou and simultaneously come up with something that won't have us strangling the substitute head of kitchen in your absence?"

"How complicated are these experiments I'll be monitoring?" It wasn't like she'd arrived up to speed.

"Not complicated at all," Lou assured. That, Janine was to discover, wasn't quite the case. Had they been as uncomplicated as Lou insinuated, Chad could have easily carried them off in conjunction with his own work. However, they weren't so complicated that Janine, with her professional background, thought she was unqualified to handle them and do a good job in the bargain.

"So?" Lou asked when she'd completed the rundown. Roger, by then, had excused himself, saying he'd check in later for Janine's final decision. "What do you say?"

"It's certainly different from anything that was ongoing at Marine World."

"The life forms are just smaller," Lou encouraged. "All the big aquatic life was wiped out by the explosion. It's surprising, though, how what was left has adapted so well and what new life—particularly algae—has taken up residence."

Janine had to admit that it was all pretty fascinating. It was just that....

"Something bothering you, Janine?" Lou sat back in her chair and eyed her friend and one-time college roommate.

Janine felt under one of Lou's high-powered microscopes.

"I just would hate to screw up on all the work you've already done." Of course, that was no lie but, more importantly, Janine was still weighing the pros and cons of holing up with Chad for forty-eight hours.

"Who got better grades all down the line in school?" Lou asked. "Who had to tutor her poor schmuck of a roommate through more than one college course? Huh? Don't talk to me about screwing up, Janine. You and I both know your qualifications. So what's really bothering you? Chad?"

"Chad?" Janine's response was too loud and too quick.

"Jeez Louise!" Lou said with a sigh. "What's the problem, there? He's single. You're single. It's obvious there's chemistry percolating between the two of you.

"I just prefer slow and easy to run amuck."

"You know, when I decided I loved—I mean *liked*...." Janine wasn't fooled by Lou's last-minute substitution. "...Jack?" Lou asked. "It was the minute the two of us met. So, don't tell me you need a six-year lead-in and equally lengthy courtship to decide you like Chad and that he likes you."

"Maybe you're right."

"Believe me, babe, there's no *maybe* about it."

"Columbus took a chance—and died in prison."

"Jesus!"

"So, that decided, I'd better get ready for lunch." Janine checked her watch. "You can stick around and see how it's done, or I can give you a more leisurely run-through later. What'll it be?"

"The leisurely run-through, later." Lou scooted back her chair and got up. She flashed Janine a *you're going to have fun* smile. "In the meantime, don't be too concerned about you and Chad. These things have a way of working themselves out on their own, if they're meant to be. You know what I mean?" She gathered up her notebook and hummed a jolly little tune as she exited the room.

"Problems?" Brad asked when Janine joined Jenny and him behind the service counter.

"I've been drafted to take over some of Lou's experiments on the North Face."

"Oh, why?" Jenny asked. Having overheard the news, she obviously didn't consider it good news. Undoubtedly, she imagined herself back cooking for a group that obviously didn't like or appreciate her cooking *at all*.

"It's really not going to interrupt our kitchen routine too much," Janine promised. "Lou will be here, substituting for me for the couple of days I'll be in and around the crater."

"Thank God!" Jenny's relief was evident on her pretty face.

"I'll work up the menus before I go," Janine said, "and make sure the recipes are pulled for easy reference. I see no reason why any of this should turn into a big deal." She remembered an omelet Lou had once made, staying over at Janine's parents' house in Spokane; it was the first and last time Janine subjected herself to Lou's cooking. Should she mention that to Roger who had obviously suffered so much under Jenny's culinary ineptitude?

"Hi!" Chad called from the doorway, interrupting. He came in and walked as far as the counter, leaning on over it. "Busy?"

"As a matter of fact, yes." They'd have plenty of time over the next forty-eight hours.

"Okay, then, I'll leave, as soon as you assure me that you've decided to change places with Lou for the suggested couple of days."

"Consider yourself so assured." He had to be the handsomest man Janine had ever seen.

"Fan-*tas*-tic!"

"Now, we really do have a lunch to serve."

♥ *Chapter Eight* ♥

THE SCRAMBLED EGGS were runny. Janine didn't like runny eggs, scrambled or otherwise.

Her toast was cold. She didn't like cold toast.

She was less aware of runny eggs and cold toast than she might have been, though, because she was so intent upon how Chad and she would soon be off, together, in a helicopter, to the crater.

"I don't like runny scrambled eggs," Chad said.

Janine glanced up from her plate and saw him shift coagulated yellow-and-white first one way and then the other with the tongs of his fork.

"I don't like cold toast, either," he said. "It reminds me of the way the English do it. Certainly, I don't like burned sausage." He smiled widely. "Thank God, we're getting out of here this morning before everyone grabs pitchforks and comes after Lou and her two kitchen helpers for burning. Why don't we jettison this poor excuse for a working-man's breakfast and head on out to the chopper to wait for Ethan? Maybe we can steal a couple of his candy bars."

Ethan, as it turned out, was already at the chopper.

"I hate runny scrambled eggs," he said by way of greeting.

"Don't forget cold toast and burned sausage," Chad said.

"All of which leaves me to wonder if we should be flying Janine anywhere. It seems cruel as hell, as far as everyone is concerned, to leave Lou and that crew in the kitchen."

"Off bright and early, are you?" Roger asked, coming to join them.

"Have *you* eaten yet?" Chad wanted to know.

"Headed there, now."

Chad looked to Janine who looked to Ethan who looked to Chad. They smiled in unison, having decided it was time to fly out before Roger came running to put Janine back in the kitchen—experiments be damned!

"What?" Roger asked. After all, he hadn't been born yesterday.

"Nothing," Chad assured. "We'll see you in forty-eight."

Although Janine had ridden in a helicopter a few times, it hadn't been enough so that she wasn't all butterfingers when it came to figuring out the shoulder harness and seat belt of this one.

Chad didn't miss out on the opportunity to give her a helping hand, although he made sure not to take advantage.

The chopper was soon airborne, and it swerved toward the southeast.

Janine's stomach gave little lurch. At the same time, she reminded herself that Ethan had flown in the war when other, less experienced pilots, hadn't lived to return and tell the tale.

In a surprisingly few short minutes, Chad pointed below them to an orderly arrangement of buildings along a paved, two-lane highway. He said something, but Janine missed it in the roar of the rotors.

"Troutdale," he repeated, up close; although it was more a case of her successfully reading his lips than actually hearing, even this time.

He tapped on Ethan's shoulder to signal them down.

Janine thought for sure they were going to crash as the copter immediately slid downward and to the left. It seemed to be but inches from the ground when it finally leveled off and set down. She still couldn't hear well until the motor was turned off and the rotors were slowing toward their eventual stop.

"Troutdale, as I was saying," Chad said with a silly grin. "I thought, since the phone lines are still down, since the quake, that you'd probably like to advantage the opportunity to check in, right off, on your Great-Grandma's friend. See if she's all right and all."

In truth, Janine still thought that her use of the team helicopter for a social visit was something Roger would disapprove.

"Looks like we're drawing a crowd," Ethan said, turning back over his shoulder. Three boys and two old men seemed hardly a crowd, but— "Somebody better hop on out and tell them that we're not here to evacuate because of what's happening to and on the mountain."

Chad reached across Janine and opened the door on her side. He brushed her while doing so, and—right on schedule—she experienced the same thrilling chill usually got every time he physically touched her.

"Isn't this detour going to cut down on our time on the North Face of the crater?" Janine asked, momentarily not budging. If Sarah Zent found out Janine could arrive by helicopter, once, she'd want to know why the young woman couldn't fly in later. At Sarah's ripe old age, she might not understand the nuances of what was and wasn't proper usage of team equipment.

"If you have trouble monitoring Lou's experiments, I'll lend you some of my expertise, on-site," Chad promised. "Now, I think we should let the crowd—" The crowd now consisted of several more kids, another old man, and a few middle-aged women. "—know we're here merely to say hello to one of the residents. Living permanently on the side of a mountain whose other side has recently blown away, has these folks more used to helicopters arriving to bring bad news."

Janine slid out, automatically ducking her head despite the deteriorated movement of the overhead rotors. She would try to explain to Sarah why it was impossible to do this more often.

"Trouble?" one of the old men asked. "I knew there'd be trouble when the mountain moved again this morning."

"No trouble," Chad assured. The poor old boy was assuredly senile, since Chad knew of nothing that insinuated ground movement since the large one experienced when Chad had been en route to the camp.

"And the ground movement means just what?" the old guy wanted to know.

"Actually, no such ground shift turned up registered by any of our equipment," Chad tried to be reassuring.

"Your fancy equipment doesn't know squat, then" decided the old gentleman with obvious disgust. "What else is new?"

"We're here to visit Sarah Zent," Janine changed the subject. "She's a friend of my great-grandmother."

"Sarah lives over there!" one of the attending women obliged. She pointed toward a copse of evergreens farther down the road. The leading edge of a beige trailer house poked from among the trees.

"*I* say this damned mountain moved again this morning," the old man insisted, prepared to take up where he'd left off. "What do you say, Sammy?" He'd turned to the white-bearded gentleman on his right.

"Nah!" Sammy contradicted, shaking his head. "I didn't feel a damned thing."

Janine touched Chad's arm and turned him from the developing confrontation. She began walking toward the trailer, and Chad followed obediently along.

"Typical paranoia," Chad diagnosed. "I'll bet you'll find people up here who'll swear on a stack of Bibles that the mountain hasn't stopped moving since the big blow in '80."

They continued on their way and entered the trees originally seen from a distance.

On closer examination, the trailer looked as if it had seen better times. Its wheels were gone, and it was sitting on crumbling cement blocks whose disintegration had already caused the trailer to tip noticeably. Large sections of beige paint were blistered and peeling, revealing pale gray underneath.

The door opened before Janine could knock. The young woman on the other side of the screen was obviously *not* Sarah Zent, unless Sarah had found the legendary Fountain of Youth.

"Are you here because we have to evacuate?" the young woman asked and brushed a stray lock of red-brown hair off her forehead.

"We're here to see Sarah Zent," Janine said. "I'm Janine Woof, and Mrs. Zent is a long-time friend of my great-grandmother. I've just been assigned to the scientific team up on the mountain."

"I'm her great-granddaughter, Marianne. At the moment, she's off for her morning constitutional." She checked her watch. "She's been gone for a little over an hour."

"She's out *walking?*" Janine wasn't sure she'd heard correctly. Sarah Zent was Great-Grandma Woof's cotemporary—the two had been girls together—and while Great-Grandma Woof could get around on her own, the idea of *her* taking off on an early-morning walk, alone, for over an hour, in some dim-lit, possibly bear-infested, woods, boggled the mind.

"She should be back any time now," Marianne promised. "Would you like to wait? She'd never forgive me if I let you go without her seeing you." She stepped back and opened the screen.

"Maybe you could just tell her I stopped by," Janine suggested. "As soon as the phones are back on line, I'll be sure to...."

"Nonsense!" Chad interrupted. "We can certainly spare a couple more minutes."

He was already inside the trailer, and Janine—albeit reluctantly—followed.

Although Janine didn't consider herself old, there was an undeniable freshness about the younger Marianne that had Janine wishing not to be held up in comparison. The young woman had deep blue eyes, a complexion unmarred by even a single zit. Janine could only be thankful Marianne wasn't dressed in something more flattering to her figure than the plain housedress, nondescript apron, and sandals.

"I'm sorry I can't offer you anything but orange juice," Marianne said.

"Orange juice would be nice," Chad said; Janine envisioned him asking Marianne if she'd mind whipping him up some scrambled eggs, non-runny, while she was at it. Maybe some hot toast and some nicely done sausages as well.

"It must have been dark when Mrs. Zent started out this morning," Janine said to Chad and watched him watch Marianne.

Chad must have felt Janine's eyes on him, because he turned toward her and smiled all-innocence.

"Great-Grandma goes out at dawn every day." Marianne obviously had overheard Janine's question and now provided a response as well as a glass of ice-cold juice. "She says old age nor the mountain is about to stop her, especially since she's quite convinced by her visitation that she's not yet due to die."

"Visitation?" Chad asked over the rim of his glass.

Marianne looked embarrassed. Janine would have liked saving her from an answer but was frankly curious herself.

"She was on the North Face the morning the mountain blew," Marianne said and fiddled with her apron string. "She had several cabins over there and

87

was staying in one, all the tourists having pulled out because of the preliminary earthquakes. She was going to do her very own Harry Truman number—" Harry was the colorful owner of the Spirit Lake Lodge who had sworn he wasn't going to leave the mountain, no matter what happened, and was now buried beneath literally tons of ash and debris. "—but early that morning, she woke up and found an angel at the foot of her bed."

"I beg your pardon?" Chad was right on cue. If he laughed, Janine was prepared to strangle him.

"The angel asked her what she was doing there when there was still work for her on this Earth," Marianne said softly.

Chad had the good grace to take it all in with a straight face.

"The angel told her to get into her car, without even bothering to dress or pick anything up but her car keys, and drive here," Marianne continued. "She'd had this trailer sitting here for years. She and Great-grandpa used to come here fishing as a change of pace from the tourist-crowded streams around their other cabins on the North Face."

There was the sound of someone on the steps outside. In one coordinated movement, Marianne, Janine, and Chad stood up.

"Marianne?" a clear and strong voice asked from just beyond the screen.

No one in the room had any doubts who was doing the asking.

Sarah Zent, all eighty-nine pounds of her, came spryly inside to join them. She didn't have to be told who her guests were, either.

"Ah, my dear," she said, as if she'd known Janine for as long as she'd known her own great-granddaughter. She extended her hand to Chad. "And, you must be Dr. Samuels who Melissa said, and rightly so, 'is as handsome as the Devil himself.'"

"For a brief moment, Janine hadn't a clue as to the identity of the mysterious *Melissa* to whom Sarah Zent referred. Then, quite suddenly, like a flash of lightning, she realized that Sarah was the one and only person Janine had ever heard call Great-Grandma Woof by her Christian name.

HEART ON FIRE, BY WILLIAM MALTESE

♥ *Chapter Nine* ♥

WELL, JANINE BELIEVED, she had found one woman who hadn't exactly been taken in by Chad's considerable charm.

"I do believe," Chad said, laughing, "that Sarah Zent truly believes she was saved from the eruption by an angel just so she'd be here, today, to protect you from me."

Janine and Chad were headed back to the helicopter where Ethan was killing time by entertaining the local kids by letting them take turns sitting in the pilot's seat.

"She did rather give that impression," Janine agreed. Her smile was primarily the result of her embarrassment felt for the good-intentioned Sarah who had come very close to making a fool of herself. Janine could only guess what Great-Grandma Woof had imparted over the phone, before the lines had gone earthquake dead, but it seemed to have convinced Sarah that Chad was intent upon leading Janine down the road to perdition.

Thank goodness Chad had a sense of humor, or he would have certainly been less indulgent of Sarah's third-degree. Anyone would have thought he was on the witness stand for some heinous crime, Sarah the Chief Prosecutor determined to nail his sorry ass to a plank.

"She seems to have a far greater respect for my skills of seduction than I do," Chad said and watched Ethan shoo away the kids in preparation for takeoff.

Janine and Chad ducked for the resulting down-draft from the suddenly spinning blades.

Janine was thankful she wasn't required to make conversation for the next few minutes of entering the helicopter and strapping herself in the harness and seat belt—this time *without* Chad's assistance. After which, the sounds inside the chopper were loud enough to make conversation difficult if not impossible.

"Heading up!" Ethan nonetheless announced, and they were off like thrill-seekers on some carnival ride.

They headed north in an eastward curving path that, Janine assumed, was designed to keep them out of ear-shot and eye-shot of the camp. Roger might wonder what the helicopter was *still* doing in the immediate area.

"Ethan is going to take us up for a close look at the crater before he attempts any kind of set-down," Chad shouted, his mouth so sexily near Janine's ear that she felt the movement of his lips.

She watched, fascinated as the chopper skimmed tall treetops until the trees disappeared, and the south rim of the massive crater was suddenly directly below them. The 2,100-foot hole, on the other side, had been made by an explosive force estimated to have been the equivalent of 500 Hiroshima A-bombs; it was a sight to leave Janine in complete wonder.

Oh, she had seen all the newspaper and magazine photos, seen it all on TV, seen it all from a passenger seat on a commercial airliner flying at 27,000 feet some hundred miles to the north, but none of that had prepared her for the other-worldliness of the close-up reality. She honestly felt as if she'd been transported from the Earth to the moon via one of those science-fiction gismos ("Beam me up, Scotty!") that had so often dissolved, and then reassembled, *Star Trek*'s Captain Kirk and Mr. Spock.

There were no woods growing the North Face. Certainly, *nothing* grew on the new dome couched inside the pit like an egg inside a nest. The trees that had once formed forests as thick as those Janine had flown over to get there, had been toppled toward the horizon in a complicated weave and covered with dust to turn the landscape a uniform gray.

Although she knew that ecological recovery *was* in process, that there were bracken ferns, fireweed, asters, lupines, thimbleberries, avalanche lilies, trailing blackberries, and pearly everlastings in bloom down there, those isolated clumps of green were lost in the full scope of utter desolation whose main punctuation marks were deep gouges in the landscape, serrated ridges, and enormous potholes, many of the latter filled with steamy brews whose mists only occasionally shifted to show seemingly pea-soup contents. The remains of Spirit Lake, visible to the north-northeast, once turned as completely gray as the rest of the landscape by the May 1980 explosion, was beginning to regain a hint of its original blue, but that was the only visible sign of hope on the vast Hieronymus-Bosch canvas.

"We'll take a closer look at the dome," Chad said, tapping Janine's shoulder.

Ethan took the copter down on cue.

They passed through the filmy whiffs of vapor gone airborne from the hump of swollen earth below; the dome looked less egg-like than alien aircraft skidded to an unscheduled stop.

Even as Janine watched, a bright orange glow blossomed where there had been only dark rock before.

Unbelievably, solid stones from the spot levitated directly toward her.

The flung rocks *looked* insignificant only until she realized they had to be damned big for her to see them so clearly from that distance. That realization was struck home more forcefully when the first of them actually hit the aircraft and lace-like lines simultaneously appeared on the windscreen.

She'd later remember that Ethan and Chad shouted something, but she never would remember what, probably because she was so concentrated, at the time, on the sheer marvel of what she was seeing.

The chopper swerved sharply, in an attempt to make it to the leading lip of the crater, and over to the other side. All of the while, there were accompanying *ping, ping, pings* of volcano-tossed stones colliding with, and sometimes penetrating metal.

Suddenly, there was no seeing the dome within the crater. Everything below was seemingly nothing more than one boiling cloud of dust and cinders.

The helicopter lost altitude, became completely immersed within a polluted miasmic atmosphere that burned Janine's eyes and clogged her lungs.

Ethan and Chad's continued shouts still refused to register intelligibly on Janine's mind long enough, loud enough, for her to decipher. There was simply too much attending noise and things happening for any one thing to be successfully singled out for proper analysis.

Deep inside of her, Janine had the inexorable suspicion that she was going to die. It made her unbearably sad. Not because she found death so frightening, although she certainly did find it that, but because Chad and she had been unable to fully explore their possibilities for a genuine relationship.

There was a sudden darker engulfment of everyone and everything.

Janine gasped for air and choked on more dust.

There was a cacophony of sounds: Chad's sounds, Ethan's sounds, Janine sounds, mountain-in-eruption sounds, the helicopter-being-bombarded-and-going-down sounds.

Fear? Was that what Janine was feeling? It all happened too quickly for fear. Fear was often the product of anticipation, and whatever this was had come without decipherable forewarning. *This* was just suddenly there, death a likely consequence. And, quite frankly, death might well be preferable to the tremendous heat that she sucked into her lungs, along with the dirt and the grit and the ash.

If she smelled sulfur and brimstone, which she did, both aromas attributed to Hell, she could only think that Chad and Ethan and she, in the end, should have been able to count on better forever-afters.

No denying she was surprised when the darkness temporarily swept to one side, and she realized they were still airborne. That feat seemed more and more miraculous as the metal and plastic cocoon in which she continued to reside played out its tin-can-hit-by-rock racket all around her.

They were still moving forward, too. Toward *where* and toward *what* were entirely uncertain as the darkness returned with more heat, more dust, and more nose-and-eye-burning stench.

If they hit the inside of the crater, it would be like birds hitting a plate-glass window.

Janine knew she should pray. Except, there was simply too much happening to pray.

Suddenly, there was the inside crater wall less than three feet in front of her face. Had she been able to extend her arm through the cracked and heat-blistered helicopter windscreen bubble, she could have touched the volcanic surface and brought back traces of it on her fingertips.

The rock wall slid down, and a vast slope of land slid up to fall away towards a distant gray horizon.

Up and over the lip? Safe? Janine didn't *feel* safe.

If her looking-for-the-best mind-set, assaulted as it was by negatives from each and every side, could deliver her from the suspicion that she may yet be delivered from the belly of the beast, it, also, told her that death could just as easily await her at every next second. The revealed landscape was desolate as the helicopter dropped closer and closer to it.

"We *are* going down!" And who screamed that? Chad? Ethan? Janine?

Certainly, Janine knew for a certainty that they *were* going down. The ground was simply on the rise too damned fast not to.

"Chad?" How sad that two people possibly destined to find true love should end up first finding death together.

Chad's head lolled forward on his chest. Dead already?

Janine didn't want Chad dead. She didn't want to die, either. She wanted them both to have the time they should have had to sort out what kind of relationship—if any—they would have together. It was infinitely unfair that she and he should have their free choice taken from them by a mountain that had already claimed 61 lives and was now preparing to snuff out three more.

No denying the impact that telescoped her spine, jarred every bone in her body, and rattled her teeth.

The sounds of tearing and twisting and denting metal were inhuman screeches that grated raw nerves. A sudden *Boom! Boom! Boom!* quick-filled all the available airspace around them.

Then, silence.

So, was she dead or alive? It wasn't as easy to determine as she thought it should be, because of the complete darkness *and* the fact that she was unable to move. Mentally, she seemed out of contact with any part of her physical body.

She tried to put what had happened into proper sequence: the flight over the dome...the suddenness of the mountain in eruption...the copter up and over one edge of the escarpment...the ensuing descent...the crash.

Was the present darkness part of the Hereafter? Was it the lead-in to some glorious light to follow? Was it the never-ending ethereal world of the damned, so full of dirt and dust that there would never be another sunrise?

Or, was the blackness only the result of Janine's eyes shut so tightly?

She opened her eyes to an unnatural twilight. She became even more disoriented. There was definitely something out of whack, out of kilter, askew.

Why did she look like she looked? Why did Chad look the way he looked? Why did Ethan look the way he looked? Could all of this twisted metal in which they were cocooned really be...what?

"Chad?" She looked to him to put some meaning to the madness, although it was obvious he was unconscious and wouldn't be immediately answering any questions.

"Janine?" It was Ethan who was asking.

Janine wanted it to be Chad speaking her name. She feared if it wasn't, then he was dead. She didn't want Chad dead. She didn't want him seriously injured, either. How could Ethan or she get a seriously wounded Chad adequate medical attention?

"Ethan?"

What exactly was Ethan's position and condition? What, for that matter, was hers?

Jesus, they all dangling upside-down like bats!

Her sudden awareness of their hanging made her acutely aware of the blood already rushed to her head.

Ethan was first out of his harness and seat belt. There was the loud crash of his ungainly descent and scramble for more normal alignment.

Metal was bent even farther as Ethan moved some bits of crash-distorted fuselage to access Janine.

She was alive. Ethan was alive. Oh, please, dear God, let Chad be alive!

"Let me get you down," Ethan said; Janine's fingers just couldn't successfully manipulate the sudden puzzle of metal clasps that held the confining straps against and around her.

"See about Chad, first," she said. "I think he's hurt." She couldn't bring herself to suggest he was dead.

"I don't see any way of getting to him before I get you out of the way."

Her snaps released her, and she fell. Her coordination all shot to hell, she would have landed directly on her head, probably broken her neck, if Ethan hadn't been there to direct her tumble and catch her.

Once she was down, she turned her attention to Chad, and Ethan was quick to lend a hand. After only a few seconds, however, it was obvious that there was no longer enough room for the three of them. Common sense persuaded Janine to slide off to one side and let Ethan take charge.

The view beyond the immediate confines of their squashed container wasn't anything to raise Janine's spirits. It was, in fact, totally nightmarish.

All around was a gray and dusty landscape made more so by the smoke that completely covered the now-very-dim sun.

They'd crashed outside the North Face and in the blow-down zone whereon thick forest had existed until the May 1980 blast of the mountain had leveled all the trees like so many dominos gone down.

If Janine bounced up and down, where she stood, she was aware how a supporting cross work of interlaced fallen timbers, beneath the downed helicopter, bounced, too. The spring-like response might well have cushioned their fall and saved their lives, although their landing hadn't seemed even vaguely cushioned at the time it happened.

Off to her left, the crater of Mt. St. Helens, visible through the collapsed serrated edges of its North Face, was filled with a maelstrom of spark-specked blackness. The size of the mountain and its present mushroom cloud, combined with the desolation on all sides, made Janine feel small and bug-like.

Up, down, and sideways, fine dust was suspended in the air, only some of it continually gravity-dropping to powder everything. They could survive the crash only to end up suffocated beneath ash like the victims of ancient Pompeii.

"Give me a hand, Janine," Ethan called her back to the more optimistic reality of him alive, her alive, and...*Chad? Oh, Chad, please be alive!*

"His shoulder harness is really fouled," Ethan explained his slow progress, "but I think I've about got it. Just try and make sure he doesn't drop on his head when I release all support."

Easier said than done, because with Ethan and Janine crowded around, there wasn't enough space into which Chad could descend from his hang-space position, except into his resulting sprawl over Janine's back and onto Ethan's left knee.

Afterwards, they somehow managed to manhandle him outside, although he was dead-weight the whole way. Janine shuddered at the *dead* part of *dead*-weight.

She slid her fingers along Chad's neck. His skin was warm, not cold. When she felt his pulse, she started crying.

"He's alive!" She couldn't help but say it aloud.

"Well, thank God for that!" Ethan agreed.

Janine wiped the back of her hand across her eyes and came away with a streak of tears and mud.

It helped tremendously that Ethan remained so seemingly calm, cool, and collected. He'd been in battle zones before, of course, and this was definitely a battle zone. If the enemy, in this case, was a mountain and not men, that didn't make the situation any the less potentially deadly.

"Just what is your condition, do you think, Janine?" Ethan asked.

"I'm fine, but Chad…."

"Forget Chad for the moment," he insisted. "I want *you* consciously to take stock of *your* body. Chad has no apparent serious lacerations, with no immediate evidence of internal bleeding, but I won't likely know what's wrong with him—if anything—until he wakes up and tells me. But you're conscious and lucid. Shock sometimes masks injuries and, if that's the case, I want you to sort yours out, here and now. Can you do that?"

"Right!"

"Take it from the top," Ethan instructed. "Run your fingers physically through your hair and check for soreness and the stickiness of blood."

She did as she was told.

"Now, carefully check your shoulders, arms, and hands. Any broken fingers? Any serious sprains?"

She shook her head no.

He continued his running commentary, making her walk, wiggle her toes, do deep-knee bends.

When he finished his check-list of to-do's, he smiled.

"You seem to have come through pretty well for a rookie," he complimented. "Now, if Chad would just oblige by coming around, too, we could all pat each other on the backs before getting on with more pressing matters."

"I'm worried about Chad," Janine stated the obvious. "Do you think it's serious?" If anyone knew, Ethan would.

"He probably bumped his head, or something bumped it for him. Head injuries aren't easy to figure."

Janine ran her fingers gently across Chad's forehead; her fingertips located a bump at Chad's left temple that Ethan had as much as predicted would be there. Discoloration of surrounding tissue had already begun, only now evident in the dim lighting.

"If only he'd make some tiny sound." He was so silent, Janine couldn't really be sure he was still breathing until she reconfirmed by finding his pulse at the base of his neck.

"Nothing to do for him, now." Ethan was stoic. "We can only sit back and hope for rescue. Base camp knows we're in this area, and they'll send out a chopper from Cougar as soon as it's safe for them to come in after us."

The sooner the better.

Janine took Chad's hand and held it, giving it a reassuring squeeze.

His dusty fingers didn't return the pressure.

She was more worried about him than she had ever been worried about anything or anyone in her whole life.

She knelt by the wreckage, there beside the man for whom she'd come to care so deeply in such a short time, and she prayed, giving thanks for their survival and asking for oh-so-much more.

HEART ON FIRE, BY WILLIAM MALTESE

♥ *Chapter Ten* ♥

ETHAN PREDICTED THE LIGHTNING and carried the unconscious Chad to a safer distance from the downed metal helicopter. Janine followed along and staked out a place for herself beside both men and up against an exposed outcropping of rock that poked above the mat of fallen trees.

"I have to go back for some things," Ethan said and left his two companions for the return balancing act to the precariously perched chopper.

Janine scooted to cradle Chad's head on her lap.

She looked out across the expanse of landlocked logjam, fearful for the scrambling Ethan even if he seemed perfectly cognizant of what was needed for him to do what he was doing. Janine wished she were as confident as he was.

The buildup of static electricity continued. Janine's skin tingled with it, and she became genuinely concerned for Ethan who was now scrounging around within the metal of the wreckage.

When the atmospheric fireworks began, Janine couldn't believe her eyes. Never in her life had she seen such a close-up display of so many streaks of yellow and blue-white light crisscrossing the heavens in so many different directions and angles, sometimes all at once.

Flames thrust first one way and then the other, providing bursts of brightness, like day, within an otherwise dimness that was going darker with each moment from more floating ash and smoke.

Janine was sure she saw flickering blue outlining the helicopter wreckage at the very same time a particularly large stab of brilliance split the sky with an accompanying sonic boom.

In the darkness, made darker by the preceding blast of brilliance, Janine was temporarily unable to see anything.

She was afraid. As long as she could be assured, though, that Ethan was alive, she was confident he would, somehow, if humanly possible, see all three of them to safety. Were she to be left alone with an unconscious Chad, she doubted just the two of them would survive.

So, *was* Ethan still alive and, if so, where in the hell was he?

Another lightning bolt traced the exact path of the one just before it; so much for lightning never striking the same place twice! There was a sudden clamp of something, over and onto Janine's arm. Her accompanying scream was completely drowned out by the loud crashes of thunder that attended two more slashes of white-light across the sky.

She grabbed for whatever crawled her arm; undoubtedly, it was some denizen from the netherworld summoned by the hellish incantations that rumbled the mountain and bathed each and every thing in eeriness.

Embarrassedly, she discovered it was only Chad's hand which now rested on her arm, without her having seen him lift it to get it there.

"Chad?"

The next flash was a blessing in that it gave Janine the light she needed to see that Chad's eyes were open, the magical gold of his gaze somewhat glazed, but....

"Hey, Babe," he asked, wondrously able to see her, too. "What's up?" So much for the stereotype response of all those once-revived: *"Where am I?"*

She leaned over and kissed his lips, unable to help herself. Albeit dusty, the kiss was one of pure joy.

He groaned twice as she helped him into a sitting position. No matter his outward appearance, he obviously hadn't been left unscathed. At least, though, he was conscious. At least, though, he was alive.

"Ethan flew us out of the crater, but we've gone down in the blow-down area," she said.

"Where is Ethan?"

Sweet Jesus, yes, where *was* he? Janine had lost track.

"He's at the helicopter, trying to find anything usable." She refused to believe Ethan had come this far, only to have been electrocuted. "He should be back any minute."

"Actually, he's back, now," Ethan said and materialized on Janine's right. His naked torso was revealed in another flash of light.

If he looked downright skinny when dressed, his chest and stomach were actually a maze of deeply defined and well-delineated muscle groups.

"Hey, Chad, welcome back to the real world—as hellish as it turns out to be."

He deposited his discarded shirt, which he'd converted into a carrying sack, into a niche in the rock.

"How are you feeling by the way, buddy?" he wanted to know.

"A headache," Chad admitted.

"You whacked your head a pretty good one. Double vision?"

"Not at the moment."

"Any other major aches or pains?"

Janine was confident, from personal experience, that if Chad had any that Ethan would ferret them out.

"I'm afraid my leg is a bit screwed up." It was the same leg Chad had injured in the earthquake. "This isn't exactly the kind of therapy Hank ordered."

"Your shoulder?" Ethan, as well as Janine, remembered that Chad's shoulder had suffered damage in the earthquake as well.

"Pretty much the same as before." Chad rolled both of his shoulders to test for any discomfort.

"What about gut pains?" Ethan asked as calmly as he'd asked Janine when she'd performed for his checklist.

Chad was none too quick with a response.

"So, where does it hurt?" Ethan was quicker on the uptake than Janine. He didn't sound nearly as concerned, though, as she suddenly was at that moment.

"A *slight* something, here." Chad rested the fingertips of his right hand against the lower right quadrant of his abdomen.

Ethan unbuttoned Chad's shirt and peeled the material back to reveal the man's chest and stomach.

Janine shivered at the exquisite beauty of square pectorals and washboard abdominals that looked so perfect but possibly concealed a dangerous and possibly deadly flaw somewhere beneath.

Ethan pushed down on Chad's fingers which, in turn, pushed down on Chad's belly. When Ethan released the pressure, Chad's face clouded with obvious discomfort.

Chad groaned, and Janine painfully sensed all of the willpower he had probably put into not making that sound.

Ethan refastened the bottom button of Chad's shirt, and Janine took over the re-buttoning from there. Her fingers grazed Chad's bare stomach and chest as she concealed them beneath the material.

His body *looked* so healthy, so perfect. Janine didn't want to believe it was anything else but. However, she'd seen the pained expression on his face. She'd heard his telltale groan.

"What exactly is his problem?" she asked Ethan.

Ethan shrugged. "Could be a lot of things. Pulled muscle. Internal bleeding. Appendix."

"Probably a pulled muscle," Janine told Chad. It just *couldn't* be anything else. Internal bleeding or a damaged appendix sounded way too serious, considering how far removed they were, at the moment, from medical assistance.

"Probably," Chad played along with a cheerful grin.

"Definitely nothing that won't hold out until rescue." Ethan, too, was prepared to be optimistic, but there was something about the way he said what he said that didn't quite give Janine quite the assurance she wanted, needed, and hoped for.

"It does look as if the mountain is summoning in additional cloud cover," Chad said.

For the first time, Janine noticed that the non-stop lightning bursts were dimmer than they'd once been. She'd assumed it was electricity finally in decline.

"More cloud cover will make it more difficult for anyone to find us, yes?" she tried to keep her voice calm, cool, and collected. If she succeeded, it was purely façade. Their lives could very well depend upon how quickly helped pulled them off the mountain.

"They'll find us," Ethan assured.

Janine, though, glanced again toward the heavens, seeing no blue sky, seeing even less evidence of an already dimmed-to-near-invisibility sun.

"A combination of real clouds and ash could sock us in here for days," she said, made uncomfortable by the probability of just that happening. How many times, during the history of the mountain's recent volcanic activity, had she read or heard that observations were *made difficult* because of *unfavorable weather conditions*?

"I've salvaged some food and some water." Ethan ignored Janine's dire forecast. "I even found a couple of candy bars to sweeten the pot. Unfortunately, though I looked far and wide, no sign of our Coke."

"You and Janine go ahead and eat something," Chad suggested. "I'm not hungry."

"You *have* to eat!" Janine hoped she wasn't getting hysterical. There was something about the shrillness of her voice, up at least an octave from where it normally was, that she didn't like.

She'd come way too far to crack now. Doing so wouldn't help any of them. It was just that she hadn't seen Chad through this much to see him fade away just because he decided to make sacrifices that gave Ethan and her extra bites of chocolate.

"If he's not hungry, he can always eat later," Ethan said. That sounded logical. Except, there was something—once again—about the *way* he said it that carried more emphasis than his words.

Nor did Janine miss the furtive glance Ethan and Chad exchanged before including her.

"If Chad has any kind of stomach injury—" Ethan said, and Janine could sense he'd finally decided to come clean. "*If*," he emphasized, apparently disturbed by the expression on her face; Janine could well imagine his fears that he'd soon be stuck with an injured man *and* an hysterical woman. "—then, it's probably better he hold off eating or drinking anything for as long as he can."

"Of course." Janine consciously willed her heart to be still. Surely, she and Chad hadn't come all of this way to end up their days on a rock in the middle of a powder-dusted carpeting of fallen trees, lightning laser-beaming the sky, a mountain billowing black smoke, locked from rescue by a cloud cover socking down around them as securely as any burial shroud.

She felt closer to Chad now than ever, her initial attraction even more cemented by their having survived the crash together.

There was no denying that there had been a certain something that had existed between them from that very first moment she'd spotted him at the picnic table in her parents' backyard. And that something had only been reinforced and built upon by the earthquake, the kiss over milk and sweet rolls, the more intimate kiss beneath the moonlight, and the dusty kiss beneath the presently dimmed sun.

She went back to worrying about Chad's possible internal injuries from which people were known to die even when not on the side of a mountain that, for all intents and purposes, might well be literally about to blow—and for not the first time.

Janine was determined to savor whatever remaining moments Chad and she now had. Why analyze the *why* of them when they could be so short-lived, no others on the possibly catastrophic horizon? *If* they got out of this alive, *that* was the time to figure out what it all meant—if it meant anything at all.

"It's going to be all right, Janine." Chad took her hand in his and squeezed it reassuringly with his strong fingers.

How often she'd squeezed *his* hand when he'd been unconscious, hoping for even a fraction of the pressure he now returned with such ease. At least, he was conscious. At least, he was alive.

"I've waited way too long to find you to lose you now—in a bang not of our own making," he assured her with a good-natured smile.

She tried her best to smile back.

"Rescue will be here any minute," she said, her words sounding hollow in her ears and deafened by continuing atmospheric and ground rumbles, creaks, crackles, moans, and groans.

♥ *Chapter Eleven* ♥

NIGHT CAME WITHOUT a rescue helicopter or an airplane even heard over and above the prevailing sounds of a mountain in major disorder.

Black became blacker, and then blackest, ripped by non-stop frequent slashes of lightning.

Janine wasn't even sure it was after nightfall until Ethan said it was and added that it was likely all search parties had been pulled back until morning. His Rolex watch had fared their misadventure far better than Chad and Janine's less expensive timepieces.

"At least it's doubtful we'll freeze to death," Chad said, still trying to make the best of their obviously deteriorating bad situation.

The temperatures, all around, *were* high, not to mention muggy because of moisture-laden clouds which had joined the dusty swirls. Janine was constantly reminded of how it was in a greenhouse, except here there were none of the accompanying exotic and beautiful plants in attendance. This landscape remained barren, bleak, desolate, seemingly sterile, and smelling of Hades.

She let Chad's arm that was around her, pull her closer.

She laid her head against his shoulder but wasn't likely to go to sleep. How could *anyone* sleep with the very rocks oozing heat beneath them, the sky on fire overhead, the mountains liquid interior rumbling every second?

Except, always an exception to every rule, Ethan slept like a seeming baby. Lightning flashes revealed his face strangely relaxed. His naked chest regularly and evenly contracted and expanded with exhalations and in-draws of dust-saturated breath.

How many wars would Janine have to fight, how many hours spent sitting beneath this volcano, before she became jaded enough to sleep through the possibility of death so close and in relentless prowl?

♥ *Chapter Twelve* ♥

WHAT WAS THERE, those three hours later… what mysterious warning signal that simultaneously went off inside all three victims…that had Janine, Chad, and Ethan suddenly wide awake and turned as one toward the mountain's hazy silhouette in the gloom directly to the south of them?

Janine gasped audibly as a new more intense red glow expanded until the crater of Mt. St. Helens, visible through the serrated edges of what remained of its collapsed North Face, seemed lit by an additional maze of colored spotlights turned on from within.

"It'll be all right." Chad hugged her more closely.

But how could it be all right when, like the tipped cauldron that Janine had once seen at Kaiser Aluminum's Mead pot line, during a high-school field trip, the mountain began its slow spill of fiery contents?

"Oh-ho!" Ethan's startled understatement emphasized Janine's worst fears.

A river of magma was on the move toward them.

Chad wasn't nearly fit enough to get out of its way on his own. Nor did it seem probable or possible, either, that Ethan and Janine, together, or separately, could carry him far enough, fast enough, to save him.

♥ *Chapter Thirteen* ♥

"WE'RE FARTHER FROM the crater than we seem," Ethan tried to reassure.

It sounded to Janine like ongoing rationalization for his insistence that they stay put, little chance of a successful get-away in a darkness made surprisingly darker by the glowing river of molten metal approaching from the distance.

When sunrise finally arrived, not alleviating the darkness by any means, but making the air opaque enough to distinguish objects better, there was no doubt in Janine's mind that Ethan was preparing to move out.

"No one is going to find us in these conditions, unless they've help with coordinates," he said. "Our position is no longer viable for just waiting around—if it ever was. If the magma has momentarily stopped short of the blow-down area—" Yes, Janine realized, the lava flow *had* stopped, at least for the moment. "—we're going to be in even worse shape if it starts flowing again," Ethan continued. "These trees have laid around long enough so that they're going to light up fast and furious when a match that big touches them.

I'm surprised there haven't been more fires, what with all the flying sparks and lightning strikes. Possibly, the thick dust covering everything isn't conducive to ideal combustion, but wood is wood is wood and won't hold out against magma forever, even if that wood is thoroughly dusted. So, if we're not done in by the lava, we'll be exposed to the resulting fire. If the lava and fire don't do it, we'll be asphyxiated when the resulting smoke adds itself to this already lung-clogging atmospheric mixture."

Janine looked out over the maze of fallen and twisted tree trunks that Ethan proposed be traveled over and through before there could even be a chance of escape.

"Chad can't possibly make the attempt," she said and knew she wasn't telling Ethan anything he didn't already know.

"Of course, he can't," he confirmed. "We'll have to leave him as comfortable as possible and come back for him once we reach help. Once I've a helicopter at my disposal, I'll bird-dog it back here, set down, and pull Chad out of the literal line of fire."

"Set down a helicopter *where?*" Janine asked. She'd been thinking all along that, even if rescue did arrive, the helicopter would have to hover and lift them out on ropes or cables.

"Set it down, right there, of course." Ethan pointed.

Janine couldn't stifle her shiver of disbelieve. What Ethan was pointing out as a potential landing pad was the summit of the rock outcropping against which they were holed up. At the most, the space to which he referred, precariously tilted in the bargain, was less than eight feet by eight feet.

"It'll be a piece of cake," Ethan assured, "compared to some of the pick-up spots I've had to deal with in the military."

Never doubting his skills as a pilot—he had gotten them out of the crater, hadn't he?—Janine nevertheless suspected his proposal was impossible. What's more, there was no way she could go with him and not lessen whatever chances his military expertise gave him for survival.

"I'll make Chad and myself as comfortable as possible until you get back," she realistically volunteered.

"Janine, you've got to go with him," Chad insisted. He'd been lying quietly up until then, his eyes shut; Janine had hoped he'd sleep until she could get Ethan safely on his way.

"Let's *do* be practical, shall we?" she argued. "I'm not prepared to stay behind *just* because I think you need some kind of nursemaid or moral support. I'm merely increasing all of our odds for getting out of here alive by assuring Ethan the best chances of *his* getting out for help. He'll be nothing but slowed down by having me hanging around his neck each step of the way."

She raised her hand to keep Chad from interrupting. It didn't escape her notice that she was getting no argument from Ethan who obviously joined her in her assessment of their situation.

"If I went with Ethan," she continued, "he'd probably have to leave me somewhere along the line when it became plain I couldn't keep up. I'd rather be left here with you, and have company, if you don't mind."

They were distracted by momentary additional fireworks from the crater. Columns of liquid metal slopped upward, breaking at their thinning upper edges into colorful droplets that cascaded back from view. At any moment, the brew bubbling in that natural cauldron could overflow even more of its viscous contents; the river of lava, now stopped, would be on the move again and cover whatever the remaining distance necessary to ignite the blown-down timber laid out, like kindling for a fire, all around and under then.

"I'm not in shape," Janine admitted, although it was an admission she didn't relish making. "I got breathless that night you and I took a simple walk, didn't I?" That was the night he'd kissed her, and she'd kissed him back. "I'd never make it across there." She waved an emphasizing arm toward the gargantuan carpet of splintered tree trunks. She didn't add that she had her doubts about Ethan making the journey even in his obviously prime physical condition.

"I wish you'd chance it, anyway," Chad argued. He wasn't looking any too good. Oh, he was still the most attractive man Janine had ever seen, but that wasn't what she meant by *good* in the present context. Janine was pretty sure he'd taken a fever during the night, even if the high external temperatures had her hoping—please, dear God!—she wasn't mistaken.

His golden eyes had a glazed quality that made her worry that his head injury was more than he was letting on.

It didn't help any that the potential danger offered by a possible internal injury kept him from eating and drinking.

Janine had finally succumbed to hunger and to Ethan's insistence, and she'd eaten half a turkey sandwich and swallowed a few mouthfuls of precious bottled water. Thus, depleting the skimpy provisions Ethan had salvaged from the wreck.

Ethan pulled his shirt and its contents from the niche where he'd stuffed them. He laid them on one of the tree trunks that supported them from beneath. He untied the bundle as he'd done the night before when he'd pulled out the turkey sandwich and divided it between Janine and him.

"We'll divide the food three ways," Ethan said.

"Two ways," Chad contradicted. If he was sinking, he still had his wits about him at the moment. "You forget that I'm on a diet for health reasons."

Janine couldn't help wonder if it would be worse starving to death or screwing up a damaged stomach by eating. She decided the latter was worse. Bible prophets, not to mention Gandhi, among others, had often gone on long fasts and recovered from them.

"You'll be using up far more calories than I will," she told Ethan, moving two of three candy bars from her pile to his. "If I get weak, I can collapse where I stand. You'll have to keep moving."

Ethan broke one of the returned bars in half and returned one of those pieces to her pile. "I want you functional when I get back," he said, aborting all argument.

He picked up the bottle of water.

"Dividing one bottle of water is going to be more difficult," he said.

"You take it," Janine said, seeing that as the only feasible solution. If they had any hope of getting out of there, it rested entirely with Ethan and with God. God didn't need water, but Ethan did.

"Take a nice big swallow, then," Ethan offered her the bottle. "I insist," he said authoritatively when she hesitated. "And I do mean a *good* swallow. It's going to have to hold you over through some pretty hot times. And it's liable to get only hotter around here before it gets cooler."

She took one good drink, strangely thirstier afterwards than before. She recapped the bottle and passed it back to him.

"I'll try to be as quick as I can," he said and added the water to the pack he'd made of his shirt. He perspired. Droplets of his sweat converged across the top of his chest and drooled down the deep groove formed between his pectorals.

"I still think Janine should go with you," Chad injected. His face screwed up in noticeable discomfort as he shifted himself into a higher sitting position against the rock.

Ethan seemed seriously to consider Chad's final plea. God help them all if he agreed!

"Janine?" Ethan asked. Was he really willing to risk his chances by dragging her along? If he was, she wasn't.

She shook her head.

Curiously, she watched him unfasten his bundle yet again. What he brought out this time was a Bible.

"I'm loaning this to you until I get back," he said. "It belonged to a dear friend of mine: a really nice guy. I mean, *everyone* but the enemy liked him. He'd enlisted and really liked the war zone. He did his job and did it damned well. He saved more than one life, my own included, by being right where he should have been and doing right what he was supposed to do at the right time."

Ethan's eyes took on a distant quality, and Janine expected he was looking through her, seeing that other time, that other place, to which he referred.

He shook his head to clear it. His voice, which had gotten softer and more dream-like in the telling, returned to normal.

"He got himself killed by a sniper," Ethan said, swiftly.

Janine suspected there was a good deal of pain for Ethan in the telling.

"While he was dying—I mean, I knew he was dying, and he knew it, too—I asked him why in the hell it had to be him. He was the only really religious one of our bunch, and don't let anyone ever tell you that war makes converts of *all* soldiers. The notion of no atheists in foxholes might have been true of World Wars I and II, but recent wars have made more atheists out of Christians than vice versa."

Even the mountain had the good grace not to interrupt. St. Helens sat large, forbidding, and foreboding, but silent, with only a faint attending glow visible within its cupping crater to hint that it wasn't yet through with any of them.

"Anyway, I asked him why *he* had to die," Ethan continued finally, "and he said we all had to die—

sometime. Catholics, Christians, Jews, atheists. I've still never quite forgiven God for taking him, and, I guess, that's just something God and I will eventually have to straighten out between us. All that's pertinent, here, is that there are never any guarantees about when and where we go down for the final count."

Janine knew what he was saying. If she stayed with Chad, she could very well die with him. There was nothing that said for certain that she could hope to survive with him. If her time had come, then it had come. Granted, she still had the opportunity of free choice, of choosing for herself whether to go or to stay, but she could just as easily die out there in the gloom with Ethan as here with Chad. Of the two men who might be with her at the end, she preferred that it be Chad.

Last night, cuddled beside Chad, there by the rock, aware that the sweat on his brow and soaking his shirt was as much the result of his inner temperature as it was of the heat and the humidity around them, she had finally admitted to herself that she loved him. She didn't know how the miracle had happened in so short a time, especially since she *had* fought against the seeming improbability of it having happened.

But suddenly faced with the death of either of them, or both of them, at any moment, false denials of what she felt for him were suddenly ridiculous. Having found love, and admitting finally to having found it, made the prospect of her death a bit easier. Better to savor and enjoy the sweetness of love than to pretend it doesn't exist, especially since she couldn't really believe any of them was going to get out alive.

"Hurry back, Ethan." She was surprise by how calm she could sound. "We'll keep the home fires burning, in one way or another."

Ethan retied his shirt so that the sleeves and shirt-tails were somehow joined to make straps. He slipped the improvised pack onto his back.

"I don't think Chad would mind you giving me a quick kiss for good luck, Janine," Ethan said. "Would you Chad?"

Janine kissed him—albeit briefly.

His lips were dry and tasted of dust.

He smiled, saluted smartly and left.

She watched him thread his way along the cat-walks formed by the toppled timber.

"You were never that free with your kisses around me," Chad said, his voice gently chiding.

"That's because there was always the likelihood of far more complications to my life from *your* kisses," Janine confessed and walked to sit down besides him.

She didn't resist when he wrapped her waist with one arm and pulled her close. The time for pretense was over.

She wondered if he was in good enough shape for—

Quickly, she discarded any sexual fantasies as entirely out of the question, under the circumstances. It didn't matter that they might die without consummating their love for one another, with a physical union, but she could live with that. Hell, she could die with that.

"What could you have possibly thought complicating about *my* kisses?" Chad asked, seemingly all innocence.

"Okay, I love you," she told him. He might as well know it before they both died. If he didn't return the emotion, that was okay, too.

"Well, I'm glad to hear that," he said, "because, as it turns out, I've loved you from the very first moment I set eyes on you."

He kissed her, and she kissed him. Oh, she did enjoy the wondrous sensations of his lips so sensuously pressed against hers.

"I'm afraid you love a man not much competent, at the moment, to court you with anything *but* kisses," he apologized and pulled her tighter to kiss her again.

"We have plenty of time," she told him, although she doubted he believed that bit of bravura any more than she did.

♥ *Chapter Fourteen* ♥

WHAT MAGIC THE WAY the wind (or some other atmospheric force) shifted clouds and dust to reveal the patch of blue sky!

With the break in the weather, there came the first real ray of sunshine, although diluted, that Janine or Chad had seen since before Ethan had left two days before.

More welcome yet was the accompanying breath of air that seemed dust-free even if it wasn't.

"See, things are looking up," Janine encourage cheerfully.

"Right!" Chad said. Anyway, that was how Janine interpreted it by reading his lips. The sound he made, in reality, was undecipherable.

As if embarrassed by his unseemly croak, Chad shut his eyes and either feigned sleep or went to sleep—Janine couldn't tell which.

His lips were dried to the point of splitting into blood-red cracks. His tongue was swollen, his face dust-covered and gaunt as death itself.

It was Chad's steadily deteriorating state that kept Janine from a more acute awareness of her own less-than-adequate physical and mental well-being.

She sat close to him in order to keep her eyes on him. Often now—she wondered if he noticed *how* often—she'd feel for the pulse spot on his neck to make sure his heart was still beating.

She opened the Bible that Ethan had left with her, and she took advantage of the better light to read. During the varying degrees of light available over the last couple of days, she'd taken to reading aloud, because the sound of her voice gave her, and she hoped Chad, decided comfort.

As she read, she kept her ears open for the sound of an airplane or a helicopter. If she held out little hope of Ethan having gotten through, the break in the cloud and dust cover, as small as it was, meant the rescue teams could at least see them if luck brought them anywhere close.

She stopped reading and surveyed the sky above, surprised to notice that other holes in the gloom were now admitting rays of light to crisscross the landscape like spotlights at a rock concert. The effect was weird and unsettling. Besides which, the sunlight she'd so happily welcomed was making her only hotter. The way it glared down upon her, there was little shade. Suddenly, she worried that, among other things, Chad and she might suddenly end up with sunstroke.

"Chad?" She put the book aside. "Chad?" Why was she more and more surprised each time he opened his eyes? "Maybe you should take off your shirt and use it to protect your face from the sun. Do you think, between the two of us, we could manage that?"

He tried his best to unfasten his shirt buttons, but his fingers obviously weren't up to the task.

"Let me." Janine was frightened by how difficult it was, even for her, to perform the usually simple task. In normal times, she could have completely dressed and undressed him in less time than it took her to get his five buttons undone.

The exquisite muscle definition of Chad's chest and stomach seemed out of place in those surroundings. It simply didn't go with Chad's face which, while still surprisingly handsome, was haggard and strained.

By the time they got as far as getting his shirt off, the sunlight was gone, garroted out of existence by a closing in of the cloud and dust around it.

She rolled the hard-won shirt and used it as a pillow for his head.

She picked up the Bible but—whether because of the contrast from sunlight to gloom, or because the returned dimness was simply too complete, or because her eyes were failing under the strain—she couldn't make out the printed words.

She started to cry. She didn't want to. What's more, she knew it was a waste of precious body fluid.

On the other hand, she deserved a good bawl and suspected it would make her feel better when it was over. She'd held out a long time without shedding a tear, but something about the continuing hopelessness of Chad and her positions, only emphasized by the short-lived break in the weather, signaled her need for some kind of major catharsis.

She wasn't sure how long she cried before she felt the reassuring pat of Chad's hand against her arm. She looked at him, and her heart went out to him.

She pulled herself together, as best as she could, for his sake.

"Sorry about that," she apologized and wiped away the last of her tears.

He continued to pat her arm reassuringly, as if telling her, without words, that things would turn out all right.

But how *could* things turn out all right?

♥ *Chapter Fifteen* ♥

JANINE SMELLED WOOD smoke, and that made it more difficult to breathe.

She knew, without even looking—she hadn't the strength to lift her head from Chad's shoulder—that the cauldron had spilled more hot metal, and the timber in the blow-down area had finally caught fire.

What had Ethan said? *If the fire and the lava don't get us, we'll end up asphyxiated*: something like that. Janine wondered if she really cared.

It might be better to just die and leave this hell on Earth for whatever awaited on the other side.

She would have willingly died if she wasn't compelled to stay grounded for Chad's sake. Despite everything, he still lived.

If Chad were to die, though.... If she felt for his pulse one of these times and couldn't find it.... Well, then, she *would* die, too, and willingly.

Living was so painfully difficult in this pocket of Earth where the air was becoming more and more toxic, the blackness becoming more and more filled with deafening drumbeats.

HEART ON FIRE, BY WILLIAM MALTESE

No one could be subjected to so much suffering for so long and survive it.

♥ *Chapter Sixteen* ♥

BLUE SKY? SUNLIGHT? Yes! A dream, then? Whiffs of smoke blew in gossamer veils across that hole in the sky.

The smell of burning wood was a constant irritant.

The crackling of flames remained a distinctly loud and staccato precursor of doom in Janine's ears.

Chad was beside her. Did he see the blue? Did he smell the smoke and hear the flames?

Janine felt for his pulse and couldn't find it.

She'd felt for her own pulse and couldn't find it.

The tips of her fingers were numb and unfeeling. Or, maybe, she and Chad *were* dead, although she could recall nothing in her life that warranted her spending her afterlife in such a hellish place as this.

HEART ON FIRE, BY WILLIAM MALTESE

♥ *Chapter Seventeen* ♥

HOW HOT THE AIR!

How suffocating the swirl of dust that levitated to engulf them!

How ridiculous the metal bird perched so precariously on the edge of its nest, threatening to topple and fall within the dusty breeze.

"Janine, you *do* look like hell!"

"Ethan?"

"I said I'd be back, didn't I? I said landing would be a cinch, didn't I?"

"Chad, it's Ethan." She turned to Chad who wasn't there.

So, this was a dream, after all. No Chad. No Ethan.

"Chad is already in the chopper, Janine. All we have to worry about, now, is getting you inside."

She hadn't seen him put Chad in the helicopter! Surely, she would have seen him if what he'd said was true.

"Tell me Chad isn't dead, Ethan."

"Chad isn't dead, Janine."

A lie? She didn't care. It was enough, at least for the moment, to give her the incentive to take his hand and make the extreme effort it took to come to her feet.

♥ *Chapter Eighteen* ♥

BRIGHTNESS! BLINDING BRIGHTNESS!
Now, this was more like the life-after-death experience she'd expected. How genuinely nice was the softness of cocoon-like warmth around her.

Yes, this was *definitely* more like it.

She wondered when her *actual* passing had occurred. How had she finally died? From asphyxiation? From burning? From dehydration? From starvation? From heartbreak?

"I think she's coming around!"

The voice was familiar, but why not? Death was but a transition to meeting family and friends who had passed on before, wasn't it? Whose voice was it, then? Aunt Fran? Aunt Marta?

"Janine, thank God!"

"Lou?"

The bright lights were neon bulbs on a ceiling above her.

The shadows weren't spirits but physical bodies gathered around her.

"Lou?" she repeated.

"Damn right!" Lou's hand was cool against Janine's forehead.

"Chad?" Even she recognized the growing hysteria in her voice.

She'd felt for Chad's pulse and hadn't found it.

She'd looked for him beside her, and he wasn't there.

"Chad!"

"This is going to help you sleep," someone, not Lou, said.

She didn't want to sleep. She'd just come awake!

Somebody or something held her down. There was a sharp pain in her arm.

"Chad?"

"He's fine, honey," Lou assured. "Really, he is."

The lights faded.

Janine didn't want the darkness; she'd had too much of it already.

She tried to fight its coming, but she was no more able to keep it at bay than she'd been able to summon sunlight on the mountain.

♥ *Chapter Nineteen* ♥

"**AH, YES, HERE SHE COMES.** Earlier even than the doctor predicted, I might add."

With great difficulty—her eyelids seemingly smeared with glue—Janine opened her eyes.

Ethan was sitting by her bed. Or, was it merely wishful thinking that put him there?

"I came to collect the Bible I leant you. I did tell you it was only a loaner, didn't I? But look—" He held up a *Bible* too new to be his. "—Sarah Zent gave me this one to leave with you."

"Sarah?" Things were so fuzzy. Janine couldn't get her thoughts completely wrapped around anything. If Ethan hadn't chosen that moment to thump the *Bible* with one hand, she would have doubted it, or he, was really there.

"Actually, it was Sarah's great-granddaughter who gave it to me to give to you," Ethan confessed. "You remember Marianne?"

For Janine, it was hard remembering *anything*.

"I went over to Troutdale to tell Mrs. Zent how you were getting along," Ethan said. "She and Marianne asked me to stick around for dinner." He looked suspiciously like a little boy caught suddenly with his hand in the cookie jar. "Would you believe I stayed and actually enjoyed it?"

"Tell me this isn't a dream." If it were a dream, it could have been far worse.

"No dream!" Ethan assured. "I would have been in there to pick you up off the mountain sooner but by the time I got out, I wasn't making too much sense; something about some of the mountain's toxic gas that I'd inadvertently ingested. It took me a good day to get my wits back. Sorry about that."

"You landed the helicopter on that mere tabletop of rock?" Janine wasn't at all sure it had happened. Remembering it somehow didn't make it so.

"A piece of cake," he said modestly. "It was the least I could do once I found out that I'd been in the dispensary for six whole hours before realizing what end was up."

She didn't ask about Chad, although it was *only* Chad she wanted to hear about; she was afraid the news would be bad news. She didn't want or need to hear anything bad.

♥ *Chapter Twenty* ♥

WHO SAID TIME HEALS ALL WOUNDS?

Janine had something to say about wounds of the heart.

After six months, she was daily confronted by things that triggered painful memories of Chad.

Mt. St. Helens had erupted yet again—big time—making nation-wide headlines. Dr. Roger Lewis's research facility was utterly destroyed. Luckily, though, everyone had vacated the premises, forewarned by Janine, Chad, and Ethan's ordeal on the mountain.

Janine had resumed her original job at Marine World which had finished refurbishment during her recuperation.

On TV, she watched a gymnast take off his shirt; she saw Humphrey Bogart kiss Ingrid Berman in a re-run of *Casablanca*; she saw one of the main characters wounded on a popular TV series. They *all* reminded her of Chad.

Even the bad Seattle weather, sprinkling rain as she drove through it to church, reminded her of the cloud and dust cover that had surrounded Chad and her on the mountain.

She'd taken to attending church regularly lately. Something about her experience, in the jaws of death, on the mountain, had left her with a hole that her re-acquaintance with *things* spiritual had a nice way of filling.

Now, there was the letter from Ethan in her purse. It was only willpower that kept her from reading it for the umpteenth time and marveling at its irony.

He was going to marry Sarah Zent's great-granddaughter, Marianne.

Everything had been so much simpler for Janine when death had been so ominously looming for Chad and her up on the perilous side of that erupting mountain.

Afterwards, it became less simple.

She'd recovered from her ordeal with a swiftness that surprised her and the doctors.

Chad's recovery was slower.

Janine several times flew down to Portland where Chad had been airlifted for special care under the personal guidance of a specialist in internal medicine. He'd been too drugged to even know who *he* was, let alone know who *she* was.

When he *was* finally able to converse, he was continually being wheeled away for some kind of test or for physical therapy.

When he was transferred to the Menur Rehabilitation Clinic in Tempe, Arizona, where visitors were looked upon as distractions for every patient's recovery, Janine had been left wondering where and what Chad and her relationship was, and/or if there still *was* a relationship. She was confused…and saddened…and uncertain…and downright miserable.

She daydreamed all through the first part of church services.

She was only vaguely aware of new members and visitors being introduced from the pulpit. Galen Wilks had just risen from his seat, a few pews down from her.

Janine knew Galen. Just moved to town from Akron, Ohio, he was now at Marine World as an assistant oceanographer.

Galen sat down.

"Dr. Chad Samuels," said someone over the loudspeaker.

Janine's head, along with everyone else's, turned in unison toward the back of the chapel.

There Chad stood, with wide smile and deeply dimpled cheeks.

He nodded pleasantly in Janine's direction and then sat down.

Everyone turned back toward the front, except for Janine who couldn't believe her eyes.

Chad brought his right hand, palm forward, up before his chest, and wiggled his fingers in kind of a *hi-there-Janine* wave.

Janine turned back to the pulpit.

Her heart beat so fast that she though it was going to leap right on out of her rib cage. She genuinely wondered if she were hallucinating.

After that, she didn't have a clue what was going on, church-wise.

Actually, she was surprised to find she hadn't imagined Chad who *was* waiting for her, calm as could be, when services were over.

"Hi," he said.

"Hi." She was on the verge of tears, so glad to see him.

He hadn't changed. Not even the rigors of his ordeal on the mountain, and his lengthy medication regimen, and his long physical therapy, had made him any the less handsome. But then, even at his very worst—his lips cracked, his face and hair gray with volcanic dust, his eyes glazed over with fever, his body internally damaged—he'd remained the most handsome man she'd ever known or seen.

"Why didn't you call and let me know you were coming?" she finally accused.

"I know what they say about separation *making the heart grow fonder*, and that was certainly the case in *my* case. However, when my senses finally checked in, one-hundred percent, I came to the realization that my doctors had rather boxed me in for weeks on end. I was afraid that, maybe, you'd moved on with your life. I thought it would be fairer to find out, in person, what was going on, rather than have you try and put it into words over the phone."

"I'm glad you did."

"Having parked outside your place, trying to get up the nerve to head on in, I just happened to spot you on the way out, and I followed you here. What say the two of us take a drive, maybe out to Alki Point, maybe stop for lunch?"

"Yes, please."

"Shall we go in my car and come back for yours later?" He took her arm, his touch as electric as she remembered, and eased her across the road to his sports car which was some kind of foreign model she didn't recognize, all shiny black and obviously expensive.

He opened the door for her, on the passenger side, and she got in. He joined her inside the car.

"So, how've you been?" he injected into the silence that accompanied his skillful maneuvering of the vehicle out of its parking spot and onto highway pavement.

It seemed ridiculous to Janine that the two of them seemed to be having more difficulty talking now, after all they'd gone through, than they'd had when they'd first met.

She thought to tell him she'd been just fine, thank-you-very-much, but she hadn't been fine. She'd spent too much time trying to figure out where their lives and relationship had been, was, and was going. She'd been too frustrated with how she would have preferred everything made easy and not made so complicated by his lengthy recovery, and by doctors who didn't have a clue as to how some healing powers weren't found in a bottle or on a therapy table.

Janine regretted that she hadn't just set her foot down and marched right on in, proclaiming to one and all, doctors and therapists included, that she was this man's woman and no one was going to keep them apart, come hell, high water, internal injuries, or physical therapy. No way had Chad been in any condition to be so assertive.

Had she been allowed, or had she insisted, to be constantly by his side, it could well have been a bonding experience to last them for the rest of their lives.

Did he, like her, blame her for not being forceful enough to have been there for him?

What had there been, about his long recovery, and her exclusion from most of it, that had made things, now, different and difficult? Or, did things just *feel* different and difficult?

He steered the car into one of the marked parallel parking spaces along the beach. Because of the cool temperatures and recent rain, the walkways were pretty much deserted.

"Let's walk," he suggested.

She opened the car door and got out. He joined her.

"I *know* I should have come to Tempe more often," she said, glad finally to be out of the cramped confines of the auto.

"Maybe not," he surprised. "Maybe you did just the right thing. I needed as much a chance to sort things out as you did. After all, how long had we known each other? Three days? A little more? A little less? Not long at all to be proclaiming undying love for one another, was it?"

Once Janine had gotten around to admitting her love for him to herself, she'd never again questioned *that*. Not then. Not now. Not ever. Her dilemma—and failure—had been in trying to decide what to make of it after she'd admitted to it. It hurt her deeply that he might somehow have come to think of his love for her as something too spur of the moment to be counted significant.

"Although, actually, it was plenty long enough for me!" He stopped in his tracks; automatically, she was brought to a stop beside him. "My feelings for you haven't changed, Janine," he said and turned to take her

146

shoulders in his hands as if he feared she was about to run away from him.

She wasn't going anywhere.

"These last months," he said, "have done nothing but give me time to reconfirm that everything I said, everything I felt, was right and valid. On the other hand, I realize that you might need a little more time, and I do intend to give it to you. I'm just back in your life to spend whatever time is needed to convince you, and all the Woofs and Farnwells, Great-Grandma Woof, even Sarah Zent included, that I'm truly worthy of you."

"I *do* love you," she said and found it not half as difficult to get out as she'd imagined it would be. His being there made it genuinely right and easy.

"Really?" He actually sounded surprised.

"Jeez, you really are an ass not to know it."

"And you think we can convince your extended family that I'd make you an A-one husband? You *are* going to say yes to marrying me, right?"

"Oh, Chad!" Her voice cracked. She was very near to tears.

She wrapped her arms tightly around his powerful neck and drank in the pure wonder of his hard body against her. She basked in the pure magic radiating from his black-flecked golden eyes.

"That was a, 'Yes, Chad, I'll marry you!', was it?"

"Yes, Chad, I *will* marry you. I thought you'd never ask."

Her heart was on fire with the love she felt for and from him.

Tears unashamedly washed her cheeks.

He kissed her long, hard, full and deep.

HEART ON FIRE, BY WILLIAM MALTESE

As she clung to him, and he clung to her, her heart and body thrilled with the wonder of the miracle.

The cloud cover opened above them and spilled bright and glorious sunlight whose resulting rainbow symbolized the final end to whatever the previous possibilities for more storm.